GAIA AND LUNA

In the View of the Moon

Mark Newton

LOUDHAILER BOOKS

This first edition published in 2021 by:

Loudhailer Books
13 Lyminster Avenue
Brighton
BN1 8JL

www.loudhailerbooks.com

For Kai, Geo, and Maya

Bang! And then there were scalars and vectors and particles; fundamental particles that were infinitesimal, but super-hot and careening in all directions with dizzying velocity. As they ran, they cooled, and still moving with incredible speed, began to coalesce, radiating to all points as they did so. Primal forces strained to sow the seeds of a something new, sorting the fundamentals into protons and neutrons; and the elements of matter were born. On they sped, ever outward, relentless in pursuit of order from the chaos of their genesis. Neutrons met protons, and then lassoed electrons into their orbit; and then there was mass.

Cooler and cooler, but still super-hot, the big G stepped in to demand more. Now the G had something tangible to work with; to benevolently guide, mould, and create. The implacable reach of G desired gas; and it was so. The big G wanted nebulae, and they came to pass. The architect grew bolder, forcing the reluctant matter to compress and nucleate until it yielded and burst into effusive balls of light. The epoch of basic force was at an end, and now, with infinite patience and dexterity, the recalcitrant matter was cajoled, herded, and submitted to the will of the G.

Bit by bit, and through eons of time, spinning disks of matter were carefully aligned, and then meticulously compressed, around the massive furnaces of fusion. Amidst a cornucopia of different shapes and forms, great spheres were fashioned to spin and turn at the behest of their conductor in a glorious symphony of creation that travelled ever outward in a timeless mechanism of celestial beauty.

And in one imperceptibly tiny part of one of the countless galaxies that the big G kept in order with deft and subtle influence, a thoroughly unremarkable star was sparked into existence. This cauldron of fusing elements was neither a giant nor a dwarf, but the G had commanded that a number of spherical pebbles should be scattered to turn around it; something that the G did not accord all of his fiery offspring. Some were big balls of gas, some were smaller lumps of rock and iron; some were hot, others were cold; some the G regaled with magnificent ring systems and multitudinous mini-pebbles of their own; and some he left to plough their furrows all alone.

So it was that Gaia, the third stone from this entirely average star, came to be. Her birth was just as tumultuous and fiery and violent as any other, and from the jetsam of her own creation, at least that was what they latterly supposed, the G bequeathed her a sole diminutive companion, Luna.

For eons they danced around each other, as they danced around their star, gazing in undiminished awe at the cosmos, patiently awaiting that time when the Sun — for that was the name of their star — would reach out and take them into his fiery embrace. For all this time they were but the most ordinary and unremarkable components of the creation of the G to be found anywhere, but this did not bother them as they complied with the gentle but unrelenting impulse of the creator.

Infancy was not easy for either of them, but especially for the first born, Gaia. Luna, being much smaller and more simply constructed, cooled faster and found herself a solid and robust stability relatively quickly.

Her older sibling, however, was for a long time convulsed and twisted by the raw energy of her incandescent heart. Such pressures she endured, as the writhing mass of her soul sought to defy its containment. She cracked, spewing her fiery insides to her surface, then healed, and then cracked again as she tried to calm her inner currents and mediate her fluidised energy toward equilibrium.

For a very long time, Luna could but look on and try to soothe her sister through her reflected glow and the gentle caress that was all her diminished mass could muster. At times she was horrified by the constant fire and brimstone shape-shifting of her big sister, the vast eruptions with their immense plumes of gas and the tectonic shifts that continually rent and tore at her surface. But throughout all of Gaia's growing pains, she remained steadfast at her side, growing to love and admire the fiery energy and indomitable spirit around which she orbited.

Further eons passed, and slowly, ever so slowly, Gaia grew up and began to master herself. She was still subject to many an upheaval, but they were of progressively diminished frequency and magnitude; and with her growing calm and assurance came further changes that once more astonished the small, but solidly dependable, Luna.

All of a sudden, or at least it seemed to her, being accustomed to measuring time in eons, Gaia turned into a beautiful blue and white pearl surrounded by the delightfully thin and delicate halo of her atmosphere. Luna did not have one of those. The big G had not permitted her to hold on to gases, so small was she, and she wondered what it must feel like to have one. Gaia tried to explain the sensation but, as Gaia she had always had an atmosphere, and Luna had never had one in the first place, Luna never quite felt that she could understand entirely.

But she was not capricious or jealous, and simply marvelled at the curious properties of this wafer thin sliver of gas that covered her sister. It had always been there, perpetual in its dynamism and often lit up in parts by huge dendrites of electrical charge. There were less of those now — but oh, how Luna loved them! And, whilst no less dynamic, this strange covering seemed to have softened, become more serene and gentle, as her sister calmed down. It appeared so slight and thin and fragile, but it could disintegrate all but the largest of those bothersome lumps of rock and ice that often rained down upon them both out of the enormous void of space. How she loved to watch as these pests careered to their doom in streaks of yellow and orange, and sometimes reds and blues and violets. She could not do that, and just had to endure the constant peppering and occasional massive thump that the big G had decided was to be her lot.

But above all it was the blue that had lately come to adorn her sister that she found so overwhelmingly beautiful. There was nothing remotely like it in their little system, or in the heavens, as far as she could see or could remember. Gaia was not entirely blue of course, nor static in her appearance, and there was still turbulence aplenty at her surface. But compared to what had gone before, Gaia's appearance had settled into a relatively gentle and multi-facetted dynamism that was a constant source of wonder to her ashen and largely invariant satellite. The blue was marbled with constantly changing whites, and beneath those Luna saw that it was punctuated by browns of all shades, which the blue constantly overwhelmed and then receded from. All that constant change bewitched the little moon and there was never dull moment to be had when regarding her big sister.

And to round things perfectly off, Gaia had grown a pair of rather natty white caps around both of her poles that grew and shrank repeatedly over time. Yes, her companion was quite the most remarkable, not to say stylish, Sun-wanderer in the system, whatever the jealous carping to the contrary of the obnoxious Venus. She was so, so beautiful, and Luna was so happy to be her companion and friend.

When not caring for, insofar as she could, and watching over her older sister during her growing pains,

Luna spent a lot of time simply contemplating the vastness and beauty of the space they inhabited. She listened to the rhythms of radiation and other phenomena that came to her from all directions; strange and ancient beats that covered the whole of the electromagnetic spectrum, and overlapped to create some decidedly curious effects. They had always been there, but these days she had become so accustomed to them that she found that, more and more, she actually had to listen for them and home in on their varied rhythms and tonalities. What they were, and what they were trying to say, consistently eluded her, but she was happy they were there.

But it was their immediate locality that she had studied and interacted with the most. And what a rum bunch they were, she had discovered, all ceaselessly turning around their Sun in their own inimitable, not to say idiosyncratic, ways.

There was little Mercury. So small and so close to the Sun, it barely seemed possible. Nobody knew how he had ended up there — or if they did, they had never let on about it — and a lot of the time she could hardly see him. She had, however, over the eons, understood enough to decide that Mercury was a decidedly odd little fellow. Of all the larger wanderers that circled the Sun, he alone refused to turn on his axis as he orbited. More than that, there was to be no simple orbiting for him, oh no! He circled the Sun in a decidedly eccentric manner and even precessed!

Mind you, she did not turn either, and always presented herself in the same manner to her sister. She did not understand why, and just considered that this was the will of the G; and who was she to question the creator? But at least she orbited in a regular manner, as far as she could tell.

But the really curious thing about Mercury was his refusal to enter into any form of dialogue, at least in any way that could be comprehended, and no one could remember ever having successfully communicated with him. For the most part he was completely silent, but every so often a sort of babbling, which was occasionally punctuated with the odd shriek, could be heard coming from his vicinity. All that those who had, on occasion, tried to interact with him had received for their efforts were bursts of further incomprehensible noises, the tone of which strongly suggested that they should desist. And so desist they did, and Mercury was left alone.

Quite why little Mercury was like that, she had no idea. There must be reasons for this sort of aberrant behaviour, but they were simply beyond her ken. Perhaps, Luna had thought, that being so close to the Sun and not rotating might not be such a gift from the G after all. That he must be so constantly hot on one side, and so cold on the other, did not seem at all healthy to her. Then there were all those other things that the Sun ceaselessly spewed out in various parts of the electromagnetic spectrum. At such a close proximity they must be very intense, and might they have addled his mind over the eons? She also noted, however, that he had no companion, and had had to live his strange life entirely on his own, forever; and surely that could not be a good thing?

Then there was Venus. Another lonely wanderer who did nothing to dissuade her that companionship was a very good thing indeed, and that she was very lucky to have her sister. Venus shone brightly, and even sparkled with a silvery shimmer that Luna sometimes thought was not so different to that of Gaia. She too could also appear blue, but not the blue that Gaia had now manifested. More than that, however, Venus flatly refused to countenance any civil interaction with a mere satellite and tirades of acid comments and abuse was all that Luna had ever received for her troubles in this respect. Sensibly, Gaia, who was also often on the receiving end of Venus's mad, often incomprehensible, but ubiquitously unpleasant, rants, advised Luna not to bother, and to just ignore her. Gaia also told her that Venus had an atmosphere as well, and that once upon a time it may have been a bit like hers. But, with time, it had changed radically, and perhaps that was why she was perpetually spiky and hot-tempered.

Whatever the case, Luna did not like Venus, and thanked the G that she had not ended up circling her. She had a certain beauty, that was for sure, but it was but a reflected, hollow, beauty that belied a deeply unhappy and lonely character; or so she thought.

Then, beyond them, there were five other principal inhabitants of their solar system, in orbits of progressively larger dimensions.

The closest was Mars. To look at him, you would think he too was perpetually angry about something, all red and striated as he was, and he also sported caps of white. But just as Venus's shiny coat belied her character, Luna had found that Mars was nothing like one might have thought. He was very relaxed, liked a chat and a laugh, and even tended toward the philosophical in his musings on the universe. She had, from time to time, however, detected a sort of melancholy about him and, as with so many things, she knew not why. But she was a polite little moon, who did not like to pry; they all went through their phases after all.

That said, Luna had found that Mars was the most learned of their neighbours, most likely as a result of his sitting at the interface between the inner and outer Sun-wanderers. By his own admission he was not terribly magnetic, or even atmospheric these days, but he did know a lot. He also had two satellites, Phobos and Deimos, of whom he was very proud, and whom he loved to bits. There were rumours that Mars's two little moons were not actually his, and that somehow, long ago, they had adopted him, or vice versa. But no one could remember for sure and, whatever the case, it mattered not at all.

It was true that, like Mars himself, they were both rather small, and one of them, who was a decidedly odd shape, babbled away in a language that was only comprehensible to his brother and the odd little gaggle of planetoids that followed Mars about at a distance. That little gang were too small for Luna or Gaia to see, but occasionally they could hear their leader, a seemingly feisty little thing called Eureka, as she and Deimos conversed. Mars had, however, informed Luna that though she looked like a right little hard nut, she was rather sharp for a planetoid, could speak the language of the major wanderers, and was certainly no fool; adding that perhaps that was why Deimos had a bit of a thing for her, if she knew what he meant.

Needless to say both Luna and Gaia liked Mars the most of all their neighbours. Most of the time he was close enough for them to communicate without too much delay or having to shout, and he was never angry, rude, or just downright nasty like Venus. And Mars was only too happy to pass on what he knew of the outer planets, who were so far away, and so very different to them, that having any sort of sensible conversation was really difficult.

The gas giants, Jupiter and Saturn, seemed very much preoccupied with themselves, but being so far distant you could hardly reproach them for that. Jupiter was the brightest and most massive of them all, and to Luna seemed to be constantly in some sort of flux. According to Mars, Jupiter had been a contender for star-hood once upon a time, but he hadn't quite made it and the G had been unable to spark him up. He was sanguine about that, it seemed, but always very quick to remind anyone who would listen that were it not for his massive presence, none of them would be where they were today! Other than that he seemed to pass most of his time contemplating his own turbulence and inner magnetism, with which he was rather well endowed. He was also in possession of a whole horde of satellites that skittered around him; and keeping track of them clearly took a great deal of effort even for such as massive fellow as he.

Much the same could be said for the more distant Saturn, though she was nowhere near as massive as her neighbour. She also had a gaggle of satellites to take care of. She was, Luna was told, of demure and gentle character, but rather taciturn and not easily given to conversation. Upon her, however, the G had seen fit bestow the most magnificent of adornments in all the system: a glittering crown of rings, which shone and sparkled like nothing else.

Then there were the ice giants, which was the term Mars used to described Uranus and Neptune. The reason he did this, he had told them, was that although they were principally comprised of gases, they also had a lot of different sorts of ice. As such, and in the opinion of the mighty Jupiter, they might be relative giants, but they were not of a sufficient gaseous purity to command the prefix that was reserved for himself and the demure Saturn. Mars had thought this a trifle pedantic, not to say rather snobby, but he did have a responsibility to be precise when relaying the information he had. Gaia and Luna could not help but agree and always made sure they thanked him for his rectitude.

Uranus, it turned out, was another strange fellow. He was a uniform and pale whitish blue, as bland as bland could be. It looked like the G had seen fit to have given him a good old rub-down back in the day, and then forgotten to apply any polish. The rumour was that his appearance gave one a pretty good idea of what he was actually like, and that he was completely devoid of any character or expression. This surprised Luna greatly, as he too had been bequeathed a little tribe of satellites that trailed around with him and so was never alone. More than that, he also had rings, though they were nowhere near as magnificent as Saturn's. Neither Gaia nor Luna could understand how one who had received so many gifts from the G could be so insipid. Then Mars had told them that, unlike any of the other wanderers in their system, Uranus spent his whole life lying on his back, and that his magnetic field was all wonky. Jupiter, needless to say, thought that this was a most regrettable state of affairs, and not at all becoming of a giant of any kind. And whilst neither Gaia nor Luna, nor Mars, appreciated Jupiter's way of speaking about this poor fellow, they had to admit that such a strange disposition could hardly do much for one's demeanour or spirit.

Neptune, the second of the ice giants, was difficult to find, even though he was a giant. Not only was he so far away, but he appeared a deep blue that was not so easy to pick out against the prevailing darkness of space. Apparently, he too maintained a tribe of satellites and had some rings, but they were all far too faint to be able to tell much about them. He also had a rather unusual magnetic field, which again did not endear him to Jupiter. "What was it with these distant wanderers?" he had complained to Mars, not seemingly to realise the irony of his statement to his red neighbour. "Something dashed odd about the both of them. But at least the fellow spins the right way up, none of that recumbent nonsense of his brother. One should be grateful for small mercies, I suppose."

Lastly, in respect of the major astral bodies, the wisdom of the all-powerful G had demanded a curious symmetry of their little system, for their realm was begun and terminated by two decidedly odd little fellows: Mercury, nearest the Sun; and a strange little dwarf that Neptune referred to as Pluto. He was even smaller than Mercury, so Mars had told them, but somehow he had five satellites that followed him about. What was more, and a bit like Mercury, he was possessed of the strangest of orbits, all out of plane, and with an eccentricity exceeded only by the comets. As a result, every so often he would audaciously sneak past Neptune and slip inside the orbit of the ice giant! "Got to admire his chutzpah, cheeky little blighter!

But really, I am not sure he is actually one of us, you know," was the opinion of Jupiter; and indeed, it was the case that no one really knew where Pluto had come from, and there were suspicions that he had been an incidental latecomer from 'outside', and not an original creation of the G.

Then there the asteroids. They were, according to Mars, barely sentient, left over swarf that Big G had piled into a belt in between himself and Jupiter. To Luna they seemed to be a dreadful rabble, stumbling about and bumping into one another every so often. Not that Luna minded, outside of the exigencies of the G it was a free universe after all, and by and large they meant no harm. But every so often one of the imbeciles would fly out of their orbit and before you knew it, bam! It had disintegrated itself by ploughing into Mars, or Luna, or incinerating itself in Gaia's atmosphere. Not really dangerous, or actively malicious — that was understood — but just so terribly inconsiderate and stupid. What had the G been thinking?

The asteroids, mind, however stupid and clumsy they were, had nothing on the meteorites. Of all of the G's creations, and spiky Venus aside, it was these menaces that Luna really did not like at all. Not only could they be quite sizeable, and carrying G-only-knows-what from wherever they came, but they had this ability to creep up on you, and were almost impossible to spot until they ran into you. Those sneaky little critters deserved everything they got when they tangled with Gaia, but Luna just had to accept their periodic pummelling, and that was that.

Lastly, there were the comets, who were the most eccentric of fellows. As they whizzed up and down and through the system, and sometimes beyond it, they chuntered away to themselves in some strange dialect that none of the major wanderers or their satellites could understand. Some of them came by quite often. Others, however, would only pass once every few tens or hundreds of Gaia's cycles about the Sun; and then there were some that took an absolute age to come back once they had passed. Where they went when they were not about, Luna had no idea, but she did know that, unlike the imbecilic asteroids and the contemptible meteorites, they were at least predictable, punctual, and polite enough to give you some warning that they were about.

As they careered into the locality, shedding their dust and muck all over the place as they went, and came within the warming influence of the Sun, they grew great tails as they sped on. It was true to say that, like Venus, they could be beautiful to behold as they passed through, but one could not help but think that this transient beauty masked a decidedly sad and fatalistic sort of narcissism. For Luna knew that, as with lonely Venus and Mercury, they too had been condemned by the G to a life of solitude and would never know the pleasure of a partner. The only difference was that one day they would dramatically end themselves in violent collision and incineration. It was just a matter of chance and time for them, and merely a matter of where, and with whom, they would suddenly meet their end.

Gaia advised Luna to try and think too much about these things and, when one of them appeared, to have some compassion. Yes they were dangerous, and, yes, they made a mess as they stormed around the Sun, but could one begrudge them those rare instances of stardom that were accorded them in a life that was, for the most part, spent alone in the cold and dark of space? "Were they not all the creations of the G?" Gaia would say, "and as such part of whatever greater plan the G had in mind?"

Luna had to agree, albeit grudgingly. She knew Gaia was correct. She just hoped that one of them didn't pick on her to end their existence as she was not sure she might survive the impact of a big one. She was not afraid, but she worried about what would happen to her sister if she were to be shattered out of existence by one of those idiots. What would happen to her orbit, and the delightful tilt to her axis that lent to Gaia such a decidedly debonair attitude; and would she not miss her caress? Gaia calmly replied only that it was pointless to worry about such things; it was not for them to question the greater designs of the G.

And so on they went, each content with the company of the other, as they waltzed endlessly around the Sun, two infinitesimally small components of the vast cosmic creation of the G.

Eons passed, and their lovingly serene progress continued. Yes, they were periodically assaulted by the varied jetsam of the universe, and over time these repeated assaults left Luna pockmarked all over whilst seeming to have no lasting effect on her sister, shrouded as she was in her magical cloak. The stoic Luna did not mind this so much, especially as Gaia repeatedly assured her that these unfortunate incidents only bestowed even more character to her reflected glow, and that she was the most perfect satellite anyone could have wished for.

Then, one day, Gaia said, "Luna my dear, I have something to tell you. Something I have been meaning to tell you for some time now, but I wanted to be sure before I said anything."

"Yes," Luna replied cautiously, not a little concerned that there could be something wrong. "What is it?"

"Well," Gaia hesitated. "You know, I do not think that we are alone."

Luna was confused.

"Of course we are not alone, Gaia! There's the two of us, Mars and his boys, that awful witch Venus, and all the others. What are you talking about?"

"No, no, I mean you and me. We are not alone any more. Something's happened… to me. I felt it at my surface some time ago. Initially I didn't understand what it might be, and didn't want to say anything before I was sure."

Confused by this sudden admission, Luna cried back, "Well! What is it? Are you all right? Is it serious? Can I do anything? Oh please, Gaia, tell me you're OK?"

And as Luna gazed down upon her friend, she thought that her appearance suddenly changed, she was still blue, but now her blue seemed to glow in an almost beatific manner.

"Yes, yes I am quite fine, my dear. Something wonderful has happened to me, to us. Yes to us! And now I know, sort of, what it is, I also know that it could not have happened without you. We've created something new and vibrant and beautiful!"

Luna was immediately relieved to hear that her sister was fine, but with the implication that she might in some way be responsible for whatever it was, found that she could not contain herself.

"But what is it?! What is going on with you?!"

And with a serenity that, even for the urbane Gaia was remarkable, she swooned, "Life! I have called it Life! We have made Life!"

Now Luna was really in a spin. What in the name of the G was Life? What was she going on about? And what was all this 'we' business?

"My beloved sister," she gently replied, masking the concern that had once more manifested itself as a result of Gaia's curiously incomprehensible reply, "are you really sure you're OK? Sorry I am being such a dunce, but can you explain what you mean?"

Once again, Gaia's blues and whites shifted to regale Luna with a regard of such a tender love that she could but calm down it as it permeated profoundly into her.

"I'm sorry," she said, "this must seem terribly confusing for you, but believe me, we have achieved something wonderful. Let me try and explain."

"You know what we are comprised of and how, with the benevolent grace of the G, we came to be? And that, whilst over the eons we have changed, well mostly me, our essential state has remained constant and either elemental or mineral in nature?"

Luna indicated that she did, more or less.

"Well, my state has changed recently. Not all the way through, you understand, I am still the same old Gaia deep down. But at my surface something is suddenly very different. You recall over the years how I have developed into what you see now, and how I have told you that, along with all the rocks and the geology, I have my peculiar atmosphere, and am now covered in all this water, that simple assembly of hydrogen and oxygen that has such curious properties and that makes me appear as I do?"

Again, Luna indicated that she did. How could she not? Over epochs of time Gaia had explained everything to her, as far as she could, in regards to her atmosphere and this peculiar substance that had lately come to dominate her surface; how it could be solid, vapour or liquid depending on where it was at her surface or in her atmosphere.

Solids and gases, Luna could readily understand, as even the vacuum of space was not completely bereft of matter, but the idea of a liquid, as with an atmosphere, she found conceptually difficult. She had a dim recollection of something of this nature from her very early childhood, but it had been really hot and had disappeared very quickly, not anything like this water stuff.

She therefore decided to consult Mars to see what he might know more about it and whether he had ever heard of 'things' going on within it.

"Oh," he had replied, "liquid water, eh? Now that takes me back. Yes, back in my youth I had some of that too, quite a bit of it actually. Don't suppose you remember that, though?"

"No, I can't say that I do," Luna replied. "Things were so chaotic way back then. What happened to it? As far as I can see you do not have any now," she then asked.

"Well, sadly, no, not in the liquid phase," Mars replied. "A lot of it upped and left it did, along with most of my atmosphere, a long time back. You know, when the meteorites were a really a pestilential shower. I still have a bit here and there, in my caps for instance, and there may be a few bits and bobs of it left lying about the place inside some of my rocks, but it is all frozen solid. But what was that you were saying? That there might be 'things' going on in Gaia's water?"

"Well, that is what she tells me," Luna enthusiastically replied before adding, "She's called it 'Life'!"

"Life! What in the name of the G is Life?" inquired the astonished Mars.

"Hmmm," Luna replied, "well, we are not entirely sure yet. But Gaia seems enraptured by it. Says it is giving her all sorts of wonderful sensations. Did your waters ever give you any sensations? Did anything happen within them?" she went on.

The red fellow thought for a while as his two boys zipped around him and then concluded,

"Well, not that I can remember. I can recall it was nice while it lasted but nothing like what Gaia is describing; and I am sure I would remember something as unusual as 'things' going on in it."

"Has anyone else had it? Or does anyone else have it now?" Luna quickly asked, eager to find out whether this was something that might have happened elsewhere, but secretly hoping that they were in possession of a system exclusive.

Mars replied that no, no one had anything quite like Gaia at present. Jupiter claimed that Europa, the sixth of his satellites — amidst a tribe that numbered almost eighty in all — was full of the stuff, though, being where they were, all of it at or near her surface was also frozen solid. Apparently, however, the maidenly Europa, was not to be drawn into saying whether or not there was anything 'going on' within the liquid water that lay beneath her thick surface ice.

As Mars was relating this to Luna, and just as he had further informed her that Enceladus, who curiously enough was also a number six, but within Saturn's tribe, also claimed to have a lot of water, she got the sudden sense that Mars was hiding something. This was truly shocking to her, as Mars had always been very open and honest about everything she had enquired about. But there was something in his voice, just a little tremulousness, which the shrewd little satellite picked up upon immediately. More than that, Mars also seemed to be looking beyond her, something he never did when in conversation, being a bit of a stickler for what he called 'politesse', and to Gaia. She glanced round at Gaia below and was further taken aback to find that she seemed to be signalling something in the form of a mass of clouds the likes of which she had never seen before.

"What's going on?" she addressed them both.

Silence.

"Come on. Out with it. What are you two hiding from me?"

A deep, rumbling "Errr" came back from the direction of Mars, which was followed by a more drawn out, and higher pitched "Ummm" from Gaia.

A decisive "Well" finally emanated from the red wanderer. "It's not something we like to talk about. But, a good while ago, you probably do not remember this either being so occupied with looking after your sister at the time, there was another place in the locality where water was to be found in abundance, at the surface, and in a liquid form. At least for a while."

"Oh!" Luna's exclaimed, "Where was that then? And why did you not want to tell me?"

"It's a delicate matter," Gaia interceded, before allowing Mars to continue.

A second "Well" from Mars was then followed by a short silence before an explanation was forthcoming.

"Back in the day, when our Sun was still relatively young, finding his way so to speak, he was not as powerful as he has become. As a result, all of us were a good deal colder that we are today."

Luna thought for a moment and realised that, actually, she did remember being a tad chillier in the past.

"Back then," Mars continued, "the warmth was to be found a bit closer to him, and it was Venus who was the jewel in our crown, and not so unlike Gaia is today. Full of joy she was, positively sparkled as our little princess. Not that she had had it easy you see, no, no, no! Way, way, way back, she had had to try to have a satellite of her own but it hadn't worked out. She just could not sustain it and it had collapsed back into her. She was crestfallen, but she carried on nonetheless; and just for a brief period of time her surface was blessed with this mysterious compound that Gaia now has in such abundance."

Luna was shocked and suddenly felt a sadness wash over her along with the seeds of the compassion that comes from understanding.

"But what happened? And where did her water go?" she interjected, eager to understand more.

Another "Well" followed, this one notably more reticent, and that was accompanied by a very profound sigh.

"It is still there; most of it, I suppose, just in a different form. For a while, all was well, and she had oceans just like your sister, though we have no idea whether anything actually happened within them. But, as the Sun grew more powerful, Venus got hotter. Too hot for the water and the composition of her atmosphere anyway, and things ran away from her. Before we knew it, the water started to evaporate and, along with a few other things that the heat vaporised, caused her to retain too much of the Sun's energy, and that caused more of it to evaporate and she got caught up in a horrible, horrible, cycle that caused even more heating. There was nothing she could do, and before long all her surface water was gone, her atmosphere had become the dense mass of seething acidity that it is today. It was all just too much for her, and she became deranged with bitterness and anger and hate. To lose a satellite and then, through no fault of her own, to be condemned to such a fate; to lose something so special. It all seems so cruel, so needless, but that was the will of the G. Not that she has ever forgiven the creator and his laws for that."

Luna was speechless and suddenly ashamed of herself. Had she but known, perhaps she could have been more understanding. It must be a perpetual torture for Venus to gaze next door and see her gaily orbiting her inundated sister with all the magic it now apparently contained. No wonder she was so vicious and nasty toward her and everyone else.

She still did not really understand the water itself any better though, and had to content herself with the knowledge that this strange thing existed, and that it was the primary reason why she was lucky enough to have, in Gaia, the most beautiful partner that this little part of space could muster. But she did felt sorry for Venus, and resolved to try and be more considerate toward her in the future.

"So what's going on?" Mars asked, curious as ever "What's this Life stuff then?"

Gaia, realising that their secret was out and could no longer be kept from their red friend replied,

"Well, it seems that this water, when combined with the heat from my insides, the composition of my atmosphere, the light of the Sun, and a few other things that I have not quite pinned down yet, can lead to all sorts of strange chemistry; chemistry that is really rather different to anything I have experienced before, you know, all that heating and cooling and pressure driven metamorphism and vulcanicity that you have witnessed over so much time? This new chemistry takes place in the liquid water and leads to a cornucopia of assemblies of the light elements that then react with each other to form new and different assemblies."

"And what's more!" she exclaimed. "Some of them are able to do the darnedest of things! They can replicate themselves over and over again and organise into ever more complex structures. In addition, and as far as I can see, whilst they are subject to the influence of the G, there appear to be other forces at work. Within this strange soup I have the sense that other factors may be involved in directing things. Isn't that amazing!"

"And I've decided to call it Life!" she added joyously for good measure, even though Luna had previously spilt that particular bean.

Luna's mind was spinning again, and even Mars looked utterly dumbfounded whilst he toyed with this strange new word, gently and thoughtfully repeating it back and forth to better get the feel of it. Little molecules all tumbling around in some sort of soup, getting more and more complex all the time, and making more and more of themselves and changing again as they went? Who'd have thought of such a thing! And what was this about other factors? What could they be and what might be their intentions? Luna suddenly felt herself anxious but, at the same time, she could not help but revel in this new concept.

Mars, having finished practising the new word, then could but just harrumph a pensive "Hmmmm". Yes, what Gaia was telling them was amazing, and both of them could not but help silently contemplate what all this might mean. Mars then told them that he had to go look after his satellites for a bit, but that he would like to know how these things developed as and when they had a moment. And off he spun mumbling to himself, "Life? What in the name of the G is going on?"

As soon as he had gone, Luna asked Gaia, in a manner that was both quizzical and quiet, "So, is that this Life you speak of?"

Gaia saw in Luna's wan reflection a certain consternation, and immediately tried to reassure her.

"Oh! My dear little sister, how you fret! I know it's not easy to get. I am still trying work through all this myself, but it's incredible and wonderful! No, what I have just described is just the start, there's so much more, and it is constantly changing and evolving. Actually, I am still not sure when things really became what I have now called Life. It is more than just the ability to self-assemble and replicate and proliferate and diversify. At some point pure chemistry was surpassed and something entirely new took over, and now I can feel its energy swarming all over me and... Oooooh, it feels so good!"

Again, Gaia's blues and whites shifted, and it was plain for Luna to see that she was truly enamoured by what she was speaking about.

"Please go on," she implored her. "I want to understand more. So what is it now? And what, may I ask, might have been my role in all this?"

Her larger sister thought for a moment before replying,

"I shall try and answer your last question first, though even now I do not think I can be definitive. It's just that I feel it; that your influence has been essential, along with that of the Sun, and possibly even those comets and meteorites that you hold in such low regard."

Luna frowned at the mention of those hooligans.

"Yes, I know, you don't like them very much. They are such strange wanderers who appear so alien and inconsiderate to us. But what they leave behind as they pass by, or into us, some of those products of the bizarre life they lead, well, who knows what they might engender given the right environment? I cannot rule them out as providing some sort of start from which all that I feel now might have grown under the benign influence of the Sun and your constant attention."

"Benign at present," Luna thought to herself, as a result of the recent revelations regarding Venus and the way she had been treated.

"Oh, Luna! How your influence has soothed and pleased me over the eons. I could never tell you how much that has meant to me, and now it seems to mean even more. This water stuff responds to you like nothing else I know.

By your command it heaves and rises up into massive waves that follow your passage around me, smashing against and inundating the land as it goes. Over and over it responds only to you! In you it has found a Goddess, one to whom it pays constant devotion, churning and mixing everything as it goes. Over this medium you have great power, and I therefore reason, as it is within this medium that what I call Life has arisen, that you and the Sun have latently conspired with me to create this amazing new phenomenon."

An ecstatic pride suddenly overwhelmed the little satellite, even if Venus and her sad fate still lingered in her mind. Could it be possible the she could have really had such a hand in the fantastical events that Gaia was relating to her? Moreover, that this material responded to her in such a manner convinced her that, even though what was going on seemed to be a supra-G event, it must have, in some unspecified way, been willed by the great creator, and that therefore it must be good. And she was now a Goddess! On a par with the Sun himself! Luna found she liked that idea very much, very much indeed!

As Luna mused happily upon her new found status, and tried to push Venus from her mind, Gaia continued.

"What this Life is now I can try and describe, even if I do not fully understand it myself. All that new chemistry has advanced itself to such a degree that now there are molecules whose only job it is to carry information, blueprints for other molecules, which they then create, and that all do different things. Over time, some of them they have assembled and diversified even further, and have even come together as integrated entities that then continue the process. They draw their energy from the Sun, or from myself in the places where I allow it to break through to my surface, or they consume others types of similar entities and use their energy to grow and reproduce. It's an entirely new type of existence!"

"We were born of fire and chaos, made to be steadfast and to endure until the moment when the Sun god will come to take us into his fiery embrace. These tiny things, however, were born from such a delicate mixture of light elements and impulses that they remain functional for just the tiniest allocation of time. They are bequeathed so little time that they can only continue by reproducing themselves as much and as rapidly as they can. And with each generation they change and diversify further. Oh! If you could but feel this seething rush of Life!"

At this moment Luna, returning from musing on her new status as a Goddess, chipped in, "So what are they now? How many of them are there? And how many different types? You said they were tiny, and consume each other. Well I am not sure that I like the sound of that last bit, but can you describe them at all?"

"Of course, my dear. I shall try as best I can," Gaia replied. "Well, they only exist in the water, and mainly nearest my atmosphere, where the energy of the Sun is at its most intense, and they can use some of the components of my atmosphere to grow. At present, individually speaking, they are no greater than a single speck of dust, though some of them have started to aggregate with their cousins to form larger communities. As to their number, there are already too many to count; as many as there are stars in the sky!"

"That many!" Luna thought. This was a concept she could very much comprehend, even if she had not yet managed to actually count all the stars that she could see; and she had tried, repeatedly, over the eons.

"As to their diversity, hundreds and thousands of different types all competing with each other to make their type prosper in the next generation."

"So how long has this being going on, and where do you think it might end?" Luna enquired.

"Not long. Only about a hundred million Sun-cycles," she replied, "but the pace of change is thrilling. The energy of these little beasties, their sheer dynamism and lust for development, really takes one aback and gives one such incredible feelings. As to where this new Life might go, and what it might do, I have no idea; only time will tell. Just now, I can only think that we have been truly blessed to receive such a unique gift and no more than that."

From that moment on, Luna's attention wandered less and less amongst the stars and the vast spaces in between them, and became squarely focussed on her sibling and her new condition. Now that she was a Goddess, she thought it only right and proper that she pay attention to her new devotee as it ebbed and flowed over Gaia, and within which this new and exciting phenomenon had been spawned. Mars occasionally looked in to see how things were coming along, only to go away again bewildered, and possibly regretting that he had asked, such was the tumult of information that was enthusiastically sent his way.

The flow of information was both voluminous and ceaseless. Gaia had certainly not understated the energy and dynamic endeavour of this Life. Not a million cycles passed when there was not news of more astonishing new developments in the diversity, complexity, and the sheer multitude of this rapidly growing miracle. And so, together, they watched over the new creation, nurtured it as best they could, and Luna insisted that Gaia tell her everything about what was happening at her surface.

This turned out to be an all-consuming pastime. Firstly, Gaia had to concentrate as never before to understand whatever had recently popped into existence. Then she had to find a suitable manner by which to convey this information in a form that Luna could assimilate. This was really not easy for either of them, and especially for Luna. The entire concept of change, other than that which was occasionally, and abruptly, introduced to her by the careless drivers of the cosmos, was completely new. But she was a plucky little satellite and not given to throwing in the towel at the slightest sign of difficulty. She was tenacious, held to her task, and even revelled in this new challenge. All that was going on was so alien, and changed at rates that were entirely unheard of — to the point that time itself, at least as she perceived it, seemed to have been altered and compressed by this new arrival in their lives. But she refused to let her sister down. Entirely new concepts had to be thought of, and then worked through, before an adequate and comprehensible description could be arrived at; and by the time they had done that, something else had happened and they had to start anew. But they stuck at it, to the exclusion of almost everything else, recording and categorising the rise of Life! What wonders they came to know, and what loving pride they developed for their creation.

Through their ever more assiduous consideration of Gaia's surface, Luna even came to understand that she was, ever so slowly, drifting away from her sister, and that as she did so her powers over the water diminished. The G did indeed move, or more precisely was moving her, in a decidedly mysterious way, she thought. And though she was not so happy that she was creeping slowly further from her companion, or that, as she did so, her powers over the water declined somewhat, she accepted it as the will of the creator. Indeed, more than that, she took comfort in this undeniable, at least to her, evidence, that whilst there might be other forces at work down there on Gaia's surface, the

G was still there, designing and gently pulling the strings of creation.

The massive oceans heaved less and, bit by bit, desisted from perpetually attacking and overwhelming the landmasses. A new, more tranquil and temperate epoch thus ensued, which only made the Life more ardent in its desire to evolve and spread.

In the oceans the complexity had reached new and dizzy heights. Plant and animal life, at least that was what Gaia had decided to call them, had appeared and grown into a myriad of ever larger and more complicated forms. The plants, so Luna was told, used the energy of the Sun to grow and reproduce, while the animal life consumed the plants, or each other, to create ever more complex food-chains.

And before long, Life decided that home in the water was not enough, and it charged out of the seas and rivers to take hold on the land; and within a blink of a cosmic eye Gaia changed again. To the blues and the white and the browns were added greens; greens of every hue stormed across the land and Gaia became even more beautiful in the eyes of her adoring companion.

On and on it went, feeding from the abundant raw materials that Gaia generously provided, the radiant energy of the Sun, and the constant mixing and churning of the air and the water, that still, if in a diminished way, remained obedient to the influence of Luna. Insects and crustaceans, and fish and reptiles, infested the seas. Some ventured to the land, following the plants, and others even decided that Life on Gaia firma was not enough and took to the air! Nothing appeared to be beyond the capacity of Life to achieve! And all of it was duly counted and categorised by its two devoted trustees; avid taxonomists who strained to keep up with the geometric expansion in the numbers and forms that were ceaselessly appearing, and often disappearing, with ever greater rapidity.

The very fragility of Life seemed, rather strangely, to be fundamental to its evolution. The individual elements of the Life, the plants and the animals, lasted but a moment in time. Even the very hardiest of them had but a few thousand Sun-cycles allotted to them. However, no sooner had the Life-force left them than entropy, the great dissembler, and eternal foe of the G, seized upon the remains, and returned the components that the Life had temporarily appropriated back to where they had come from. But, no sooner had that happened, the Life once more seized upon these building blocks and the whole process began again, though never from precisely the same point. With each recycle the Life changed. The changes were infinitesimally small in any given cycle, but they were there. And over countless cycles of Life and Death, some of them were found to be beneficial, and were propagated into the new generations, which were subsequently different to those that had gone before.

Moreover, there seemed to be virtually nowhere on the surface of Gaia that Life did not seemed determined to invade. From the highest of her peaks, to the most tenebrous depths of her oceans, each new generation probed slightly further, adapting as it went, to make even the most unlikely of places a home. With each new home came further diversification and the creation of societies; systems within which the different inhabitants sought to make their way by whatever means they could. They competed with each other, and grazed on and used, in a variety of manners, one another. Yet, within this never ending conflict and struggle for survival, wherever Gaia and Luna looked, a curiously beautiful balance was found to exist.

That balance was, however, periodically subject to great upheavals. Gaia still had tectonic stresses and strains to deal with, and sometimes her insides burst forth in vast eruptions that spewed molten rock and ash and gases into the atmosphere which could do terrible things to the Life present at her surface. When this happened she felt terribly embarrassed and even ashamed, and had to be consoled by Luna, who pointed out to her that this was but a natural part of the growing process and could not be helped. Gaia knew that Luna was correct; it was just that she hated the thought of destroying anything of their precious creation.

More damaging, however, were the periodic interventions that arrived from space in the form of particularly large and stupid asteroids, sneaky meteorites or, worse, a babbling comet. Over the eons this had happened plenty of times, and Gaia had started to understand why Luna had such a dislike for these cosmic interlopers. Some of the larger impacts had shaken her to the core and, in an instant, obliterated much of what had struggled so valiantly to exist in the first place.

But, no matter what happened, the Life refused to give up. Sometimes, almost all of it was wiped out, and the usually calm and charming Gaia became so distraught and angry that she was even to heard to curse the G for having allowed those awful vagabonds the right to exist in the first place. But, within an epoch or two, the Life that had managed to cling on was up and running again, proliferating and evolving once more, and reclaiming all those spaces from which it had been so thoughtlessly removed. Yes, for all its apparent fragility and individual transience, this Life was tough stuff and was not to be easily extinguished. Those that had been lost were duly mourned by the two inseparable wanderers, and the task of identifying and recording all that then appeared was taken up again.

The reflective Luna, far from just acting as custodian of these records, constantly perused, cross referenced, analysed, and thought about them. What did it all mean? The constant cycles of Life and Death were truly perplexing, as was the seemingly endless conflict between the components of the Life and the external entities that tried their best to eliminate it. She noted that each mass-extinction, far from being an end, was just a new beginning; one that offered to those who had survived new opportunities. More than that, the Life that followed these events was not just different, but was, in some way, stronger and better than that which had gone before.

The last time one of those events had occurred Luna had had to look on as a massive lump of fiery rock had ploughed into her sister to excavate an entire ocean in an instant. The tsunami that followed was of a sort that had not been seen since Luna had circled her sister in much closer proximity, and the water would rise up in vast plumes in honour of her passage. The lasting damage, however, was, caused by the debris that was blasted high into Gaia's lovely atmosphere, and which swathed her in an abominable mask that completely hid the beauty of her blues and greens for a good while. Eventually, when things had settled down, and Gaia had recovered herself, the carnage that had been wrought was duly tallied.

Even though Gaia had, in one of her involuntary and embarrassing tectonic shifts, inadvertently caused quite a few extinctions and some changes in the climate a little beforehand, she had been, at that time, particularly lush and diverse. The land and the seas thronged with the most advanced plants and animals they had thus far observed. The dominant animals of the time were huge reptiles, the descriptions of which enchanted and fascinated Luna.

Moreover, as Luna's records clearly showed, they had been around in various forms for, what was for Life, a very long time. But bam! And they were gone, along with innumerable other life-forms, both terrestrial and aquatic.

Needless to say, Gaia was inconsolable. She blamed herself, her damned tectonics, and cursed the universe for a good few hundred millennia before she calmed down. But as usual, when they reviewed the situation, and even though they lamented the passing of those magnificent reptiles, they found that someone else had taken up Life's banner and sought to fill the vacancy. A previously inconsequential group of animals, which Gaia had called mammals, had stepped into the spaces left by the giant reptiles and profited aplenty from their untimely demise.

However, as Luna had noticed, it wasn't as if extinction only occurred as the result of those ghastly external interventions, it was always going on at a much lower level. Species and families of species were always falling by the wayside as a result of something better coming along and shunting them into oblivion. She had even understood that, over the eons, and since life had manifested, the average rates of the extinctions seemed to have a precise and constant relation to the diversity present at any given time. Life and Death, so it seemed to her, were inextricably bound together in some great struggle, just as the G, the eternal lord of order, constantly battled the evil of entropy. One seemed incapable of existing without the other. But what did it all mean, she repeatedly asked herself? And why had it apparently come just to them? On these latter points, however, she could never seem to come to any sound conclusions.

Beyond these seemingly unanswerable questions, Luna noticed certain other intriguing and, in some cases, quite bizarre properties of Life.

Throughout all this proliferation, there remained this beautiful and elegant balance; nothing was wasted and everything recycled. And though species, entire families, and even orders, came and went, every element that Life created had its place within the whole; a place that would be rapidly taken up by another should the occupant of that space fall by the way, and a new opening present itself.

What was more, the Life could, over time, manipulate and alter the environments that Gaia had bequeathed to it. The plants took the lead in this Gaia-forming activity, and with their sheer numbers and global mass acted as stabilising bulwarks against any sudden environmental change of the sort that Gaia and her insides might inadvertently cause once in a while.

And then there had been that radical shift in how the more advanced and complex forms of Life had decided to reproduce. Up a point it had seemed sufficient to simply reproduce copies of the original organism; an act that could be achieved by individuals within the species. But this had suddenly been deemed outmoded, and the evolutionary avant-garde had decided upon a different course. This involved two members of the species having to come together to create the next generation, such that the offspring possessed something of both of the entities that had created them. The advent of 'sexual reproduction', as, after some consideration, Gaia had decided to call this new phenomenon, had radically enhanced the rates at which life changed and evolved. As a by-product, it also introduced new levels of competition within species that, in the previously existing reproductive world, had been absent. The right to reproduce was no longer a given, it had to be assumed, fought for, and then exercised in a completely new way; and from this, new degrees of complexity in intra-species behaviour arose, along with new sources of conflict.

Yes, however difficult and unforgiving Life could be, it was never dull, and there seemed to be no end for its desire for change. More than that, Luna thought, this Life had undeniably constructed itself into an integrated and definable system; one that was both extremely resilient and, to a very considerable degree, capable of regulating itself according to, and in respect of, Gaia's own circumstances and resources. But why was all this ceaseless change and never ending diversity required in the first place? What the point of all this was still eluded her; but what a lucky moon she was to bear witness to all of these strange events.

When, on the odd occasion that she was not completely occupied with Gaia and the Life that now ran all over her, Luna looked out into space just as she had always done before the advent of this new, and apparently highly localised, happening. There too she found a definable and integrated system of celestial mechanics, wherein everything had its place and within which there was also change. Things out there also appeared and disappeared, albeit on timescales that were radically different to what was going on beneath her, and with a much diminished diversity. The cosmos was positively serene by comparison to Gaia's surface. Moreover, the whys and the wherefores of the cosmos seemed so self-evident and simple to her. Even the existence of those damnable asteroids, the miscreant meteorites, the eccentric comets, and what had happened to poor Venus, appeared comprehensible as the will of the G.

The contrast between what was going on at the surface of her sibling, and the timeless mechanism of the cosmos that surrounded them, however, she found difficult to reconcile with the omnipotence of the G. While she had understood that the G was still present in the Life that adorned Gaia, and that she had been chosen by the G, along with the Sun, to influence and nurture this new form of existence, it was just so different. Yes, it had structure, and within that structure there was beauty and balance. But there was also suffering, and conflict, and so much Death, none of which she could associate with any definable purpose, save for the continuation of the Life. Could something be its own end and purpose at the same time? she wondered; and, if that could be so, what on Gaia did it mean, and was it at all healthy? Might there indeed be something beyond the G that had manifested itself in this strange way? Was it possible at all, and here she barely whispered the notion to herself, that this was all just the result of blind chance?

All these new thoughts she found a not a little disturbing and, as best she could, she put them from her mind and returned to her curation of the increasingly voluminous history of the curious fate that had befallen her sister.

A relatively tranquil and temperate period ensued, during which Life prospered once more. From time to time, Gaia's shifting insides still burst forth, or caused seismic disturbances that shunted and cracked her surface, and her land masses continued to move about. These, however, were but minor events in relation to all that she had previously experienced, and had little effect on the Life that she hosted. By degrees, her temperature sometimes rose, then fell, and then rose again; and whilst these perturbations did cause some types of Life to disappear, the majority always managed to adapt and carry on. During these modulations, Luna loved to watch the way Gaia's white caps of solid water grew and then receded; and then how the levels of the sea changed accordingly to, at one moment cover up, and at another reveal, parts of her landmasses.

The mammals, who had profited most from the removal of the giant reptiles from the scene, grew and diversified across the various disconnected lands that now existed in between the vast oceans; and, as she continued her book-keeping activities, Luna took a special interest in two new groups of mammals that had appeared since the last devastating act of cosmic interference. In the seas there were the cetaceans; and on the land, Luna was rather taken by a very new grouping that Gaia had named 'apes'.

Physically, these two groups could not be more different, not that Luna could see them or, indeed, had ever seen any individual that Life had produced. Luna could see a lot from her elevated viewpoint, but all the elements that Life had thus far created were just too small for her to observe directly. Gaia, however, dutifully relayed as much detail as she could, which Luna duly noted, and she then used her imagination. With all that she had learned ever since Life had appeared, Luna considered that she was now able to create for herself reasonably detailed and accurate pictures of how these animals appeared and how they behaved.

Some of the whales, so Gaia said, had developed into the largest animals that had ever existed. But, whether they were these giants of the oceans, or any of the smaller varieties that roamed the seas and larger rivers, they lived in extended family groups, within which Gaia reported what appeared to be rather complex interactions. Gaia had observed that these mammals could communicate with each other using sound waves of a particular frequency range that the water could carry great distances. Some of them even used this capacity to organise themselves to achieve certain tasks by working together.

The apes too lived in extended family groups, within which even more complex social hierarchies and interactions existed. They lived mainly in the forests and, for the most part, were relatively small tree dwellers. Lately, however, some of them seemed to have moved from their arboreal strongholds into more open, and more dangerous, territory. They also communicated with each other in a manner that was more complex and nuanced than had been previously observed. More than that, Gaia had told her that some of them had started to use implements, such as sticks and stones, to make some aspects of obtaining food easier. The apes, and the monkeys from whom they were descended, were not apex predators, and still lived rather precarious lives but, as with the whales, aspects of their social behaviour seemed to have within in them something really new.

The advent of social behaviour and new forms of organisation was yet another development that fascinated the little moon, as it seemed to owe little to any of the elementary forces that drove either Life on Gaia or the universe in general. All in all it seemed to be a direct consequence, albeit one that had taken a while to assert itself, of the invention of sex as a means of reproduction and diversification. It was also true to say that, in various forms, it had been around for a while. Many of the lower life-forms, and especially those strange segmented beasts called insects, organised themselves into hierarchical communities, some of which were, by the standards of Gaia's Life, huge. Many of the fish and the mammals had also adopted communal behaviour in order to enhance their prospects, either as hunters or the hunted. All of those developments, however, Luna considered relatively simple compared to the sorts of organisation, and inter- and intra-group relations that Gaia had indicated to her as having recently appeared. And, in the opinion of the cratered curator of the history of Life as it stood, no groups had taken this new paradigm as far as the apes or the cetaceans. As such, Luna took a special interest in them.

Before she knew it, a particular group of apes fulfilled, and then went way beyond, any expectations that Luna, or indeed Gaia, could possibly have had. With the blink of a celestial eye, they decided to do some really radical things. They shed their furry covering, became bi-pedal, and their ability to make implements out of all sorts of stuff advanced rapidly. They became voracious hunters as their tool-making and social skills advanced, and then suddenly, or so it appeared to Luna, they were on the move, colonising entire continents, and multiplying and developing as they went.

But, whilst Luna revelled in the success of her favourite apes, to whom Gaia had decided to grant a new name, 'hominids', to celebrate their achievements, she could not help but notice that their success was often not very good news for other species, particularly other large mammals. These upright, and now naked, apes had their ups and downs, as did everything else, but no matter what was thrown at them they just kept on spreading and multiplying and coming up with things that had never existed before. In no time at all they had spread themselves across almost all of Gaia's major landmasses, their societies becoming ever larger and more intricately constructed as they went.

Two of the new things that these wandering apes came up with came in relatively rapid succession were even more astonishing than their decision to adopt an upright stance and abandon the hirsute nature of their ancestors.

"You won't believe this," Gaia said to Luna one day, "but I do believe that your favourite little hominids have created language, and are talking to each other, just like you and I. Well, not precisely like you and I, but they are definitely doing it."

Luna was sceptical. "Are you sure, sister? Just a moment ago you told me that, whilst, socially speaking, they were more advanced than anything else save for, perhaps, the cetaceans, how they communicated was still far too primitive to be considered language? Next you will be telling me that the cetaceans have started singing!"

"Well..." Gaia hesitated, "actually, the way the whales do things could be regarded as a form of singing, a bit like some of the birds have done for ages, but with much more nuance and variation, not to mention being much heavier in the bass department. But I swear these hominids have actually started talking to each other in a manner that you and I would understand as such."

At this, Luna felt her craters wrinkle with both amazement and envy. How she longed to see and to hear the great cetaceans sing, or her favourite little apes talk, or even the songs of the birds that Gaia had long told her of. But this was one thing that, somewhat mysteriously, seemed beyond her sister's power.

"Oh, and there are two other things I should mention," Gaia continued. "They have started taking care of their dead, or at least to acknowledge their passing, and they have started creating things that appear to have no obvious use. You know, I think they may have become self-aware!"

The little moon was aghast and astonished in the same moment. For however many epochs that Life had been through thus far, it had never managed to create anything that one could describe as language, or indeed, self-awareness. Up until this point, these great gifts had been the preserve of the celestial bodies even, to whatever primitive extent they could muster, the asteroids. It had, therefore, been implicitly assumed that these capacities had been gifts bestowed by the G and that they were to them alone.

"What!" she exclaimed, briefly wondering whether eons of exposure to cosmic rays might have finally addled her sister's mind, before she recovered herself a bit and tried to keep the word 'heresy' from her mind.

"My dear, I do not want to question your judgement. I have never seen reason to question you, well not since you first announced your condition. But really, are you absolutely sure about this? When did this happen? It seems that hardly any time has passed since you told me they had left the forests and were still grunting at one another."

"Yes. I am sure," Gaia replied, a little taken aback, "and yes all this has only transpired in the last 50,000 or so cycles, 100,000 tops, as far as I can tell."

Much as Luna had managed, not without some difficulty, to adjust to the breakneck speed and apparent compression of time that Life had imposed upon them ever since it appeared, this seemed ridiculous. Yes, every so often there were very rapid events, such as the sort of mass extinction that had done for most of the reptiles but a little while beforehand, but language and self-awareness? How could these things have appeared so quickly?

"And what are these things that you say have no apparent function?" she asked, still ruminating as far as she was able on the magnitude and possible implications of what she had just been told.

"Well, they have started carving and daubing things, all over the place, wherever they go. Representations of themselves, the animals they hunt, and all sorts of other strange stuff; and for the life of me I cannot work out why. Sure, some of it might be created to teach others, but really the meaning behind some of the things they are making baffles me. Oh, and I almost forgot, they have also learned how to control and use fire!"

From that moment on, Gaia and Luna paid much closer attention to the hominids, and Luna spent most of her time documenting the unending streams of change and innovation that her favourite apes got up to. Both Gaia and Luna soon realised that the advent of language and self-awareness was just the start of a new age of unprecedented development within a single species; and within a very short space of time there was just one hominid species, where there had been a handful. Quite why the others fell by the wayside was never really clear to the two custodians of the ecosphere. The same could be said of the demise of the mega fauna that also disappeared in relatively short order wherever the last group of hominids turned up. But neither Gaia, nor Luna, could ever pin these disappearances squarely on this last remaining group alone.

Within a further short period of time they had spread themselves over almost the entirety of Gaia's land masses, and had gotten better and better at making tools and manipulating raw materials such as wood, and clays, and metals. Then some of them decided to stop wandering and to settle down to create permanent communities.

They continued to hunt as before but, in addition, started to cultivate crops and enter into entirely new types of relationships with some other species, such as cattle, and horses, chickens and pigs, who they added to the dogs that they had already conscripted for hunting purposes.

As Gaia looked on and relayed these events to the ever more incredulous moon, they observed that this change led to a torrent of others. The apes started shaping Gaia's surface to their own needs, cutting and burning and digging, and bending nature to their ever more demanding will. Their communities coalesced and grew with the steady supplies of food and water their endeavours realised. They even learned to produce more than they needed, and started to trade with other groups according to what materials each group might need and who had them. Knowledge was also exchanged, and language and learning developed and diversified apace. They started to build with ever greater skill and design, and some took to the perilous seas, learned to navigate, and to spread themselves, their trade, and their knowledge further and further afield. They discovered how to record and curate their ideas in a written form, and looked to the stars to discover the patterns and phenomena that defined their world. They drew inspiration from the heavens and Gaia to create systems of belief, mitigating their individual transience with collective notions that drew on Gaia's generous bounty and the startling infinity of the universe itself.

They also started fighting.

They had always been a rambunctious lot, and disputes within and between groups of animals had always been present, particularly after the invention of sex, within the ever-turning maelstrom of Life. But, as their societies and belief systems grew ever larger and more diverse, and their learning and the transmission of that learning across generations became ever more refined, conflict between them also became more and more common; and, with the application of their large brains to the art of killing, ever more efficient and bloody.

In all their time watching over their miracle of Life, Gaia and Luna had never observed any species that did what these hominids were now doing. Whilst so much of what they were achieving was a delight for Gaia to behold, and for Luna to add to her repository of knowledge, they found the increasing violence and rapaciousness of these apes toward each other and their surroundings baffling, and of no small concern.

"Why have they started doing this?" Luna eventually exclaimed to Gaia. "Why are they spending so much time and effort in killing each other? They do so many other wonderful things, why all this needless Death and destruction? Don't they realise they are all the same species!"

To this, Gaia had no immediate answer, as she did not know herself. This was a truly confounding development, not that the sudden rise of these apes to dominate her surface, or anything that they had achieved so rapidly, hadn't been astonishing. But this, on the face of it, made no sense, at least in terms of the way Life had always previously conducted itself. What had happened? What was, with ever greater frequency and levels of destruction, going on? And how did that square with all the accumulation of knowledge and the tremendous acts of creation that this remarkable species were also managing with ever greater skill and audacity?

And so they watched, not that Luna could see anything directly, and recorded. Extended civilisations and belief systems popped up all over the place, reached out, and then, often in a mass of violence and chaos, disappeared again to be replaced with something else.

Luna reflected upon this, and whilst she was starting to become concerned about the behaviour of the hominids, she realised that this was what Life had always done. What was new in these apes was that the forces and impulsions that had driven Life forward ever since they had been blessed with its presence, seemed to have concentrated themselves within this particular species: and, as they had started to master their world, they had come to regard themselves as superior to the rest of the Life that surrounded them; that they were in some way chosen, and that everything around them existed explicitly for them to exploit. They increasingly behaved, so it seemed to the on-looking Luna, as if they were the centre of everything. It was if the chaotic force and lust for change that Life had always demanded lay now only within them.

They had also started to worship an astonishing variety of deities. When this curious aspect of this behaviour had first appeared, it had seemed understandable as a consequence of their becoming self-aware, conscious of the universe around them, and their infinitesimally small place within it. Though they had no detailed knowledge of the universe, or the G, they had worshipped things that they implicitly understood as important to their short lives. Though strange, this behaviour charmed and flattered Gaia and Luna as, along with the Sun, it was they who were often the principal objects of the worship.

But lately, things had changed. The deities were being constantly reworked and recreated, but latterly, it seemed to Luna that these new idols were increasingly constructed for the explicit purpose of reinforcing the absurd pride and arrogance that had lately appeared amongst the hominids, and to place them above everything else. By and large, as it was never completely the case, the predominant religions, as they had come to be known, which had now evolved within the hominid societies, seemed to have completely forgotten about Gaia and Luna, and even the Sun. Instead, these new systems of belief invested everything in various mysterious, rather ill-defined, yet omnipotent gods, whose sole apparent preoccupation was this particular species of ape. What was worse was that the different, but ubiquitously prideful, societies who had come up with these new gods, all seemed to think that they were right, and everyone else was wrong. And with this new found righteousness came yet another reason — if any more were needed — to go to fight and kill, enslave or convert, those apes who did not share their particular opinion.

Once more, the little moon was flummoxed, and even the sanguine Gaia was perplexed, and could not explain what was going on. All she could do was to continue to relay, as best she could, what was happening, though the advent of the myriad languages that now existed made this job harder than ever before. Luna, however, seemed to be rather adept in this department. Ever eager for knowledge and new challenges, Luna loved to hear, and then to learn, all these strange new sounds, their meaning, and how they were constructed into different forms; and, typically, the modest satellite attributed her apparent linguistic aptitude as being the result of having such a fine teacher.

But, much as she loved all this new learning, and many of the continuing achievements of her upright apes, she was increasingly troubled by the other, less meritorious, aspects of their behaviour.

How could they, on the one hand, create so much beauty, and, one the other be so awful to their own kind, not to mention all the other species with whom they shared their environment? And, particularly in the former case, for such apparent trivialities as the colour of one's skin, or what they believed in, or even what gender they had been born into?

It had not gone unnoticed that one of the sexes had taken complete command of things, in a manner that seemed very much detrimental to the other, and that this state of affairs seemed to have gotten progressively worse as the new religions had developed and taken hold.

For the males to protect, to varying degrees, the females, as these sexes had come to be known, was not uncommon in the animal world. It made sense given the now prevalent strategy amongst the higher mammals to produce relatively few offspring at a time; and it was to the females that the greater part of the responsibility for this was given. But what some of the ape societies seemed to be doing went way beyond this, almost to the point of slavery, something that Luna found a thoroughly repugnant aspect of their behaviour. The sort of commensalism that had arrived with the advent of farming was one thing, but reducing the bearer of the offspring to little more than property was quite another. Even worse, by and large, this behaviour was justified through completely arbitrary, and even nonsensical, systems of belief that were the creation of the males. And if nothing else, the females did at least retain a level of the ancient recognition and regard that Life had always displayed for Luna in the regulation of their reproductive cycles, and as such she could not but help maintain a soft spot for them.

There was another thing that Luna also struggled to understand. As the apes had prospered, they increasingly seemed to regard everything in terms of 'value' in a completely different manner to anything that had gone before. What Gaia was telling her indicated that everything was now being seen as a 'commodity', though not necessarily in terms of its immediate and traditional value, but in terms of the utility it might have in obtaining something else. Incredibly, or so it seemed to the two sisters, the highest values were attached to certain minerals and metals which the apes had quickly learned to obtain and work, for no apparent reason other than they were relatively rare and pretty to look at. The apes just loved this stuff, and used the acquisition of these and other things to increase their power and status within their communities and cities, kingdoms and empires, by whatever means they could, many of which it appeared to involve the systematic exploitation and/or conquest and enslavement of fellow apes.

They had then invented something they called 'money' and created a whole system of intra- and extra-community trade based upon it. This extraordinary new concept associated value with, and therefore commoditised, everything. Worst of all, this 'money' became an object of desire in itself in many ape communities. The more of it you had, the more things you could buy and the more powerful you became. As a result, it became yet another source of conflict.

On and on it went and, whilst the two sisters continued their constant and sedate passage around each other and the Sun, the apes continued their conquest of Gaia's surface, learning and building, creating and trading, and warring and killing, with ever greater alacrity and ardour.

Centuries flew by in a moment for the two wanderers, when all of a sudden, Luna noticed something.

"I say, my dear, sorry to bother, but you seem to have something on you?" she suddenly asserted.

"Where? What do you mean?" Gaia replied.

"There, on your northern hemisphere. That place that the apes that live there have named 'China'. It wasn't there a moment ago. Looks like a wiggly scar. Have you split your crust again, or is it just a bit of metamorphism going on around there?"

Gaia thought for a moment before exclaiming, "Oh! You're right! My, I hadn't noticed, what with all the other stuff going on down here. It seems to be a wall? A great wall the local hominids have created. And you can see it!? How in the name of the G did they do that?"

Luna was also stunned. Every so often she had, amidst the constant change occurring at her sister's surface, been able to see things appear and disappear, landmasses being created or eroded away, and even sometimes things that

Life itself had actually created, most often in warm, shallow, seas, which in some places gave rise to living structures that could grow large enough for her to resolve. She was of course aware that the apes were incessant builders and, as their technology advanced, they had understood how to build larger and larger structures for whatever strange purposes they might have had in mind at any one time. But never before had anything that she could see appeared quite so quickly, or at the behest of a single species.

"What is it for?" she enquired, "is it some sort of temple again, or another ego-trip to light the way to whatever is the latest afterlife the locals have come up with?"

"No," came the reply. "It seems to have been put there to keep other apes out."

"But why so large, do you think? I mean, for the first time I can see something that these creatures have constructed. It must be magnificent close up; and they are so small! It must have taken countless of them to do that, even more than those stone circles they used to like to erect, or those pyramids you have told me about that for some reason they liked to build all over the place? And it is way bigger than any of the other walls you have mentioned, you know, like the ones those Romans built on that funny little island to keep, err, what where they called…"

She racked her brains for the right label.

"Yes, those Pictish people, those curious northerners who painted themselves blue and fought so bravely and well that the Romans had to build a big wall to keep them out! They had to build two walls in the end, if I recall." She paused as she strained to remember the facts she had learned from Gaia. A momentary silence reigned before, and not without a little triumph, "The Antonine wall! And... Errrr, yes, Hadrian's wall!" she continued, before asking, "Whatever happened to them? The Picts, I mean."

"My, aren't you the clever moon!" Gaia whooped back. "Seems your memory is as durable and reliable as you are, sister. I don't know how you do it. I am finding more and more that I struggle to remember these things. Sadly the Picts and their culture are no more; all dead or assimilated, like so many others."

"But," continued Luna, flushed with the success of her recall, "those walls were nowhere near as big, so why is this one so large? They must be absolutely terrified to have gone to such an effort?"

Yes, with all the other things they did, humans, as they had lately started referring to themselves, liked nothing better than to put barriers up between themselves and other things, and most particularly, other humans. Be it within or between human groups, they were always creating reasons to separate themselves from other apes that they, in whatever arbitrary way, did not like or were afraid of. Especially the latter, or so it seemed to Gaia and Luna. The two sisters could but be in agreement that they had never observed a species that was so afraid. They were afraid of everything: of

Death, of each other, and even of the very deities that they themselves had created. The building of walls, be they social or physical, and which had suddenly reached a colossal apogee, seemed to the perplexed custodians of Life as the ultimate expression of this fear.

As Life had developed and diversified, they had observed and noted that fear too had evolved and become essential to survival. The humans, however, had taken this basic, and essentially autonomic, response to a whole new level. It had, in them, become more than just an instinct; it had inveigled its way into their consciousness and reasoning, in parallel with the ever-more complex constructs they created, such as their societies and religions, and their seemingly insatiable desire for wealth and power. As a result, it appeared to have become more than just an emotion in them. Increasingly, it appeared to be a driver for the way they behaved and the way they put their undeniably evolved brains to work; and what they had started to call 'civilisation' and 'progress' also seemed to be inextricably linked to, and riven by, this fear.

These were but further worrisome puzzles that now occupied the moon and her sister, as they watched from on high and on low. They had nothing really to fear, save for the unwanted intervention of a random lump of rock and ice or two, and even then, they trusted in the benevolent wisdom of the G and whatever plans had been laid for them within the delicate and complex design of the universe.

"Still, it is quite pretty, at least from here," Luna stated, as they whirled onward around each other and the apes got on with their business, which appeared to primarily involve ever greater consumption and expansion, and more and more fighting and Death. Every so often, a horde would sweep from one side of a continent to the other, or, as their technology evolved, across great seas, to inflict more pain and Death and slavery upon some other poor unfortunates. Sometimes, Life had a bit of a go back, in the forms of plagues and diseases that one lot of apes had no prior knowledge of, or resistance to. They consequently died in sometimes terrifying numbers but, no matter what, the passage of these animals was irresistible, and on they multiplied, and on they spread.

Some of them, not so many in any generation or timeframe, however, did appear to have other interests. As of a couple of millennia or so, these apes had begun the process of trying to rationalise their existence and make sense of the universe around them. Others, equally rare at any one time, sought to express themselves in a variety of forms that did not involve fighting or war, or even the acquisition of wealth and power. Sometimes they were just ignored, whilst at other times these fellows might be vilified, even put to death, for their views and the expression of them; and sometimes they were venerated and respected within their communities. And it was these outliers that Gaia now took the most pleasure in telling Luna about.

They were called philosophers, poets, or sages, or artists, and they, at least in the eyes of Gaia and Luna, were a truly unique, even noble, manifestation of a possible meaning to all this Life, which, rather ironically, had appeared within a species that, for all its power and reach, seemed increasingly ugly in many respects.

How Luna longed to hear poets and music. The work of philosophers Gaia could interrogate and relay, but music was still somehow beyond her; and even though she tried to relay some of the work of the poets, Luna had the sense that, in spite her now advanced linguistic abilities, the true import of what they were saying often evaded her. It was more than just language, or so it seemed to her, and seemed to speak of more profound things. And it was far more nuanced than the relatively simple rationality of philosophy. Not that the latter did not come without questions and conundrums, and arguments aplenty, that would rumble on for centuries. How was it, she wondered, that an ape armed with nothing more than basic geometry, a few novel notions, and a stick, could have worked out that Gaia was essentially round, and had calculated, to a pretty decent degree, her size, only for this great discovery to be largely ignored and forgotten for a very long time? And, how was it that another ape, who preached nothing but humility, love, compassion and forgiveness, could give rise to a religion which had evolved into as rapacious an entity as had ever existed? An organisation which spent a large amount of its time engaged in acts of war and suppression and violence, and that spawned levels of hypocrisy and avarice amongst many of the supposed adherents to this man's philosophy that were quite unlike anything that had ever gone before? Luna noted that whenever philosophy was appropriated by religion, of whatever denomination, the 'philo' seemed to be extracted, and the 'sophy' twisted in sometimes quite remarkable and horrific ways, to become the source of so much unhappiness and suffering. For the love of the G, this Life was so trying sometimes, and these apes so dementedly exasperating.

At a different and lower level, that of pride, however, she had to admit that she liked the poets the best. They seemed to dwell on truly important matters, even if they often expressed themselves in decidedly cryptic ways. Moreover, many of them seemed to be utterly obsessed with her, took inspiration from her, and associated her with so many contrasting sentiments and feelings, that she could not help but feel just a little special as a result. And then there was this strange concept that Gaia had told her about, one that appeared from within the country that had constructed the massive wall, which manifested in a curious symbol that she could not get out of her mind, no matter how she tried.

When Gaia had found out about it, she had drawn it large in her clouds. It was circular and decidedly enigmatic. Gaia had said it was called Yin and Yang, and that she had to imagine it in black and white rather than the blue and white that she could muster. It seemed to convey a sort of balance between fundamental and opposing forces, amongst which was her good self, the feminine yin; and it seemed to contain within it something really quite profound. But did it represent a dynamic equilibrium, which could only be maintained through constant conflict and opposition, or a balance achieved through the harmony that mutual comprehension might result in? Or was it just Life and Death?

And why were there two little dots of the Yin or the Yang in the halves of the other? And, why black and white? Why so binary, monochrome, and stark? And what was going on at the interfaces between these different areas? In her now extensive experience, it was always the interfaces, the surfaces, where everything happened. This symbol, however, intriguing and challenging as it was, seemed not to be able to say anything about that, nor the insane dynamism that Life had always shown?

And then two things happened at roughly the same time that, on the one hand, amazed the little moon, and on the other, shook Luna out of her more cerebral musings and made her furious.

The first was that, amongst the philosophers, a division had emerged who devoted themselves to trying to understand the universe around them through observation and mathematical calculation. As Luna knew well, there had been always been some amongst the philosophers who had tried to do this everywhere where advanced societies had evolved. The Greeks, the Romans, the Egyptians, the Maya, the Persians, and the Chinese, for example, had all done this for various reasons and with varying degrees of success. But all of a sudden, technology had taken a leap, and the practitioners of these arts were inventing ever more precise instruments with which they could see much further, and measure things with far greater accuracy, than they had ever previously been able to do. And with these new tools they had started up-ending and overturning many of the evidently stupid, but curiously stubborn, opinions that the humans has come up with; sometimes at significant cost to themselves.

So self-important were these apes that they had, for instance, insisted on placing themselves and Gaia at the centre of the solar system, even when some of them had long since shown that this was bunk. They had also forgotten, or just expediently ignored, what the gnomon wielding, number sieving, Greek had shown over a millennium beforehand, and persisted to insist that Gaia was flat.

From time to time, both Gaia and Luna could not help but have a good old giggle at these plainly ludicrous notions. But all of that had suddenly changed, and the astronomers and empiricists, as they were starting to be known, could now demonstrate just how wrong all these silly notions were.

What was more, one of them, who resided on the funny little island where the Romans had constructed the two walls — a geographically insignificant place which had, for reasons neither Gaia not Luna could not quite comprehend, become a nexus for all sorts of things, both good, not so good, and downright bad — had come to understand something truly astounding. He had understood that the G existed. More than that, he had started to formulate, in basic terms, how the G manifested, and then use that understanding to explain the mechanics of their solar system; and, in what was a truly revelatory moment for the two custodians of Life, this ape had actually denoted part of his understanding using a big G! Now, that couldn't be a coincidence now, could it?

That joyous news related, Gaia then had something far graver to report; and, with a tenderness that was only matched by the gravity of the news, informed her that the humans had also begun to wage war on the cetaceans.

What with all the insane activity of the humans, both Gaia and Luna had not paid so much attention lately to what was going on in the rest of the biosphere. In the blink of an eye, and at the behest of the apes' insatiable need to consume and to profit, they had now turned their ever-advancing technology and navigational skills against the whales and were killing them in massive numbers. And, yet again, it was from that same funny little island that much of what was now happening appeared to have its origins.

As with so many other aspects of Life, the predation by one species on another was very much part of how this curious phenomenon worked, and, for the sake of their existence, many human societies had long hunted whales. However, what was emerging now was more than just simple hunting for the sake of survival; it was genocide! Genocide perpetrated against a peaceful, essentially defenceless and beautiful collection of beings; and for what precisely? Things, it seemed, that were, by and large, not needed, or could be replaced by other things, if you knew how to cultivate and process the right plants.

Luna was horrified; horrified and angry. She had always been aghast that the humans often tried to exterminate or suppress of enslave others of their own species, on grounds that ranged from, somewhat unbelievably to the moon: the colour of their skin; their gender; sexuality; religious beliefs; along with the simpler, but no less base, grabbing of territory and the pursuit of acquisition or wealth. Indeed, much of the latter was now being derived from that dreadful aspect of the hominid world: slavery.

That too had always existed in the hominid world but, as with the mass-murder of the whales, had suddenly become industrialised. What was more, the victims of this utterly despicable and unforgivable foundation to the most 'civilised' human societies of the time were, almost exclusively, of one colour, and derived from one part of the world.

It was horrible! And neither Gaia nor Luna could decide which of these 'commercial' activities was more disturbing and disgraceful. Both seemed anything but civil, and the stultifying levels of hypocrisy involved in the good Christian folks of the northern hemisphere brutally enslaving vast numbers of Africans, and then carting them off to who knows where to lives of misery as their vassals, were unbelievable. Both Luna and Gaia knew perfectly well what Christ had said and done. As such, that any of these greedy murderers could maintain that they were Christian was utterly baffling; though, in truth, they both knew that it was but the latest emanation of an entire history founded upon hypocrisy and the deliberate misrepresentation and exploitation of the philosophy of this man.

Indeed, in the midst of all this, a new country had suddenly appeared. Its citizens bravely rose up to fight a war to gain their independence from the most powerful imperialist dominion that had thus far existed; one that had originated from the funny little island. And having won, they then created a new constitution for themselves wherein they declared that 'all men are created equal', a sensibility that fleetingly gave some hope to Gaia and Luna. That was until they realised that this statement appeared only to pertain to the free white hominids, and not to the blacks, who thus continued to be trafficked and brutalised by their overlords in the name of profit. Nor did it seem to apply to the hominids who were indigenous to this sizeable landmass. These poor people had been systematically harried from their homelands, and then brutally pursued with guns, or by diseases imported by the good Christian humans, ever since they had appeared to blight their lives a century or two beforehand.

However, at least the other humans could fight back, and often did, being of the same stock and having the capacity to adapt, organise, and learn. But what could the whales do? They could be very large, but they had no weapons and no apparent ability or desire to fight. All they wanted to do, as far as she could see, was to roam the oceans, to live peaceful lives, and to sing.

The sheer scale of the slave trade, and the pointless bloodbath that was the persecution of the cetaceans, amongst a variety of other species, sickened both the custodians of Life. To make it even worse, the more the whales were massacred, and the harder they became to find, the more valuable the products that the apes apparently sought in them became. As a result, the mad desire to hunt them down became even greater. It was genocide at the behest of that bastard offspring of philosophy and politics that the hominids called economics, short-term notions of worth, and just plain greed.

Luna could but look on as these beastly apes rampaged everywhere. In what seemed like but a moment, scientific and technological know-how exploded as never before, and was immediately appropriated to augment the efficiency with which the humans could bring Death and destruction, both to each other and to everything around them. They powered their rampage by digging vast amounts of resources out of the ground, laying waste to everything as they did so. They declared war on the trees and deforested what they could to feed their furnaces and factories. Then they started to use the remnants of that Life that had long gone before them, the carbon they found underground and the black liquid they called oil, to create more power, more speed, and more Death, and to spew great black masses of gas and particles into the atmosphere. Even their recently attained understanding of the G was used to create ever more efficient methods of killing. War now seemed to be everywhere, and when not warring, they were massacring any number of animals on the land and in the sea. Entire species were decimated in the name of human greed, and many never came back. And, to top it all they had recently come up with a new name for themselves.

Apparently, one of the new breed of scientists, a fellow curator and categoriser of life as it turned out, had come up with 'Homo sapiens', a name that, in one of their older languages, meant 'wise man', to describe his fellow humans. Neither Gaia nor Luna knew whether to laugh or cry at this latest act of immodest pride. Clever they were, of that there was no doubt. But there seemed to be precious little evidence of sagacity in the way they behaved towards each other and the rest of the Life with which they shared Gaia's surface.

In her anger, Luna succumbed to thoughts that she had never before experienced. She may have been but a tiny satellite orbiting a small planet — as Gaia and the others that the scientists had observed with their telescopes were now referred to — in a rather non-descript part of the universe. But she had always been a happy, carefree little moon who took joy in everything around her, with the possible exceptions of Venus — though the revelations regarding what had happened to her had severely moderated her sensibilities in that direction — and the various cosmic vagabonds that occasionally raided their little part of the cosmos.

But of late, the sheer brutality, arrogance, and selfishness of this 'wise' species had started to make her fume to the point that, if she had had an atmosphere, she felt that she would have vaporised it in an instant. She found herself worrying more and more for her sister, as she understood what these 'things' were doing to her. Not that she doubted Gaia's character, how could she? She had seen her evolve, understood what she had been through, and knew that she was both sturdy and noble. But the sudden industrialised exploitation and commoditisation of the resources she had always given so freely to all of the Life that she hosted, she found appalling. "Wise men! Ha! Had such a perverse oxymoron ever been invented in the history of the universe?" she seethed. Yes, some of them had shown signs of great intelligence, achieved beauty beyond that which had previously been known, but as a collective she now thought them the very worst creation she had ever witnessed; and they showed no signs of slowing down or stopping their rapacious activities.

Dark thoughts, the likes of which she had never known, started to rise in her. "Where was a comet or an asteroid when you needed one? Perhaps she could have a word with Jupiter? She knew full well that his immense mass and magnetism could, and often did, deflect all sorts of raiders from their vicinity, and that sometimes, in a careless moment, caused asteroids to be loosed from their belt. She found herself thinking: what if Jupiter could just look away for a moment and let something through? Or, with just a little jiggle of his great magnetic field, cause a little shower? Nothing too big mind, just enough to let fly some of those moronic asteroids. Not enough to hurt her sister, and not enough to exterminate the Life she had, but enough to make these 'wise men' wake up and think about what they were doing?

Suddenly, she became fully aware of what she was thinking. Oh the shame! What was happening to her? Desist. Desist immediately, was all that she could think. She was tired. That was it, tired, and not quite herself. There was just too much going on, and way too rapidly. She felt she needed to collect herself, calm down, and talk to someone? But who? Mars was the obvious choice, but she had never before gone behind her sister's back and, more to the point, did not even know how to.

Instead, she could but gaze down upon the dark side of her sister, that part of her that, as a result of her rotation, was regularly taken out of the illuminating influence of the Sun and plunged into a transitory shadow. For eons that side of her had been truly dark, but recently Luna had observed that it was no longer so. Lights, the lights of the growing hominid cities and conurbations, had started to stipple Gaia's dark side. Initially they were but few and faint, but in no time at all, as the apes continued their incessant spread, building as they went, these illuminations had grown and grown, especially in her northern hemisphere. Now, of a night, where there had previously been but the darkness that was simply the absence of the Sun, great patches of light were now present that grew and spread in dendrites that progressively connected, to trace out coastlines and river courses, as the human societies expanded.

When she had first observed this new phenomenon, she had thought it rather pretty, something that only added to the beauty and the grace of her sister. Of late, however, as she had understood more about how these civilisations were underpinned, and all the awful things that were transpiring far below, she had start to think of these lights more in terms of evidence of some sort of infection; a disease that had taken hold and was spreading across the landmasses. Where once she had thought the burgeoning lights of the ape cities as just another beautiful adornment that Life had bestowed upon Gaia, she increasingly thought of them more in terms of psoriatic plaques, or the fractal spread of some sort of fungal or viral infection; an unsightly malady for which there appeared no obvious remedy.

Then, all of a sudden, and as if the universe had been listening to the thoughts of an insignificant little moon, one of Luna's wishes was granted, at least in part, in the form of a rather large asteroid; one large enough to get close to Gaia's surface before her atmosphere caused it to explode. In one fell swoop this moron managed to obliterate a very sizeable part of one of the northern land masses. It was spectacular, and just for a moment, Luna felt what she had previously dismissed as a rather repugnant sentiment that she had learned existed amongst the humans; that of schadenfreude. Her Yin spontaneously morphed into Yang, and for the first time in their history, she actually found herself happy at the sight of such an impact.

That was until she realised that, so pre-occupied were the apes with their latest conflicts, making preparations for their next wars, and their commoditisation and raping of both each other and various bits of her sister, they had barely noticed! Even Gaia just whooped a bit at the spank of the impact and thought little more of it. By chance, the will of the G had decreed that the impact, and the devastation it wrought, had occurred in a part of the world below that was barely inhabited and so remote that none of the humans investigated the event until years after; and even then, the investigations were primitive and perfunctory. After all, they had much more important things to get on with: such as how to best to kill those whales that remained, and endanger the existence of countless other species; how to exploit more and more of Gaia's resources, with their never-ending greed; not to mention the ideological conflicts, which seemed so beloved to them, as to how to run 'their' world.

Their technology soiled the earth, and the seas and the air, with ever greater alacrity, as they continued their apparently inexorable, and oblivious, 'progress', which not long after resulted in their getting down to the serious business of having the biggest war that they had yet managed to contrive; a world war, or so they called it.

This took place mainly in Europe, the landmass to which the funny little island, that curious source of so much, both good and bad, was but a westerly annex. All of a sudden, and following the assassination of but a single ape, they went at it for all they were worth. They fought on the land, in the seas, and even in the air, with all the new-fangled hammers and tongs that were the result of their advanced technology and industrialised methods of production. They even poisoned each other with gas! It was the biggest bloodbath yet. Millions were slaughtered before some sort of peace was restored.

Once more Luna could but look on, disgusted and appalled, at this latest act of madness. Then, as if in punishment for this latest offence to Life in general, nature had a big go back, contriving a virus that then wiped out millions more around the world. But, in spite of the huge numbers involved, barely a dent was made in their burgeoning population, one that now numbered a billion or two.

Despite, as she viewed it, the increasingly Death-laden insanity of the sapiens, Luna had, by virtue of her assiduous record keeping, made yet another remarkable discovery. In the time since this species, in its modern form, had appeared, which she reckoned to be around 200,000 cycles or so, the population of these apes had grown from almost nothing to a billion. Not the biggest number that some genres of Life had achieved, not by a long chalk, but by far the largest of the mammals. Yet, in the last hundred cycles of almost perpetual warfare, Death, and then plague, they had somehow managed to double their numbers!?

But before she even had time to relay the results of her research to Gaia, they were at it again, in roughly the same place and with many of the same players as before. This time, however, the conflict spread much further afield, and was truly a world war. "What the hell was wrong with them?" she thought as she went back to her calculations to find that in spite of all this, and in the space of less than fifty cycles, they had once more contrived to double their population!

Moreover, and just to add to her increasingly agitated state, they had also suddenly started to broadcast in specific parts of the electromagnetic spectrum that Luna could both observe and, with her accrued knowledge of their languages, understand. It was sporadic at first, but then rapidly grew into a cacophony of sound and then images. The sisters struggled to deal with this new emanation, which alongside the constant fighting, quickly grew into a bewildering deluge of often decidedly unwanted information, the likes of which surpassed anything they had known before.

Whatever their current opinions of the sapiens and their behaviour, inconsiderate and selfish being just two of the adjectives that repeatedly came to their minds, they could not help but, on the one hand, be fascinated by what was now coming their way, and on the other, more sickened than ever.

For the first time, Luna could now see and hear the nuanced complexity of these animals: she could hear their strange little voices; she could hear their language, see their art; and hear that thing she had always wanted to experience, their music. And oh my G! How she loved that music! What a truly wonderful and diverse thing; something that could express so much and seemed only to bring pleasure, make people happy, and elevate them from the mundanities and hardships of their existence. More than that, this astonishing phenomenon seemed fundamental to them, as it occurred everywhere, irrespective of race, creed, or colour! But how, she pondered, could this beautiful thing be reconciled with all the brutality and ugliness that was the flipside of these apes?

She also now heard some of their thoughts and their discussions, and saw them going about their little lives amidst the progress they were so very proud of. She also saw and heard the raging, and often incoherent exhortations of their leaders; saw how many of them acted as fearful and angry sheep at their behest; and then she finally saw, first-hand, what war amongst them really meant.

And in that last revelation, this second of their 'world wars' delivered to both Gaia and Luna something the likes of which they had never previously observed; something that was truly dreadful.

The architect of this latest conflagration, a deranged little ape who had somehow managed to rise to power, had decided that neither the extermination of other species, such as the whales, nor simple enslavement of other hominids (though he did that too), was enough. Instead, this vile little hominid had taken it into his head that what was really required was the extermination of an entire race of apes. What was more, he had managed to convince a quorate number of his fellow sapiens to go along with this disgraceful notion.

By now, man's inhumanity to man, not to mention everything around him, was all too well known to both

Gaia and Luna. There already existed in Luna's records such a shameful litany of brutality in this respect that neither of them could imagine that something even worse could be contrived; but how wrong they were! What unfolded before them, and now rendered in graphic and moving images, was so appalling, shameful, and perverse, that both the custodians of Life were shaken to their cores.

The black and white images of the 'thin people', be they the skeletal survivors, in whose sunken eyes Life seemed to have been prematurely expunged, or the great piles of twisted, barely recognisable skin and bone, which were the remains of those who had not survived what the odious little ape-man had grotesquely referred to as the 'final solution', were beyond any form of comprehension.

Luna was especially affected. Over the epochs she had thought she had seen everything. But nothing, not even those early days when she had to watch over her sister negotiate the furious eons of her fiery youth, compared to what she was now observing.

Gaia was no less disgusted, and could sense the extreme difficulty that these events were causing her diminutive, but compassionate and highly empathetic sister, and did the only thing she could think of doing.

She tried to point to all the other things they were now hearing and seeing: the music; the art; the voices of dissent; and the resistance to the madness; the courage of those who stood up to the powers of destruction that abused and selfishly exploited almost everything. But no matter the efforts of Gaia, the potent image of Yin and Yang, which had haunted the moon ever since Gaia had first revealed it to her centuries ago, now loomed larger than ever in her thoughts. Not that Gaia understood this, as for the first time in eons, Luna was silent, and remained so for, what was for her, an unheard-of length of time.

Just to make things worse, the increasingly loud and multitudinous emissions that were now coming from Gaia drew complaints from the neighbours. Venus began a strident and vitriolic rant, and from beyond the asteroid belt discontented rumblings regarding the ruckus were not long in arriving.

Mars, at least, was more circumspect and measured in his response to this rude interruption to the celestial serenity, and in spite of the horrors that he and his boys were now also witnessing, and against the backdrop of the continual torrent of abuse aimed at Gaia and Luna from the Venusian quarter, he tried to console and comfort them.

The raging global conflagration then came to a very sudden and climactic denouement. The 'sapiens' understanding of physics, through which they had really begun to understand the universe, and ask ever more demanding questions of themselves and their existence, had been combined with their engineering skills and refocused upon what appeared to be their favourite pastime: that of destroying things in general, along with those others of their kind that they did not agree with. The result was the creation of the most powerful weapon they had ever managed to realise; a terrible weapon that, for the first time, could match the destructive power of the asteroids and meteorites, and leave so much radiation in its wake that its effects on Life could last for tens, if not hundreds, of years.

One of the nations involved in this second global war, the one that appeared but a few centuries beforehand and the first to develop this weapon, decided to drop two of them on a country called Japan which, for reasons known only to the local hominids, had sided with the odious little European ape responsible for the horrors they were now witnessing.

Though Luna could not hear the two massive 'booms', this time she did not need any broadcast to tell her what had happened; she could actually feel the electromagnetic pulse that accompanied the explosion and see the huge clouds of gas and debris that they resulted in; and now it was Gaia's turn to shock her little sister.

"What the fuck was that!" she exclaimed adopting the single syllable, Anglo-Saxon, mode of expression that had, with the spread of one of their languages in particular, become rather commonplace in the hominid world. Had she not already been speechless, and still reeling internally at what they had not long been forced to observe, she would have become so, as she had never previously heard her sister utter a profanity.

Profanity existed in every one of the major languages that the apes had created, though it was generally frowned upon by the so-called 'civilised' classes of ape. Luna, however, had found it fascinating how such words, or indeed phrases, depending on the language, were so incredibly versatile and effective in communicating a whole range of sentiments, not to say actions. Indeed, it was fair to say that the linguist in her had developed a bit of soft spot for this curious form of expression. It seemed to her that it was a direct, if rather strange, reflection of some of Life's most essential aspects, such as the need to excrete or eliminate the waste products of metabolism, or to reproduce. This oddity of language therefore appeared to be a direct ramification of Life itself, as a great majority of these profanities drew upon these fundamentals processes as their foundation. As ever, however, it was the why that eluded her.

By far the most versatile and forceful of them all she thought, was this monosyllabic exhortation: 'fuck'. It could be used for just about anything, depending upon how it was incorporated into a sentence, and how the sentence within which it was deployed was relayed. And where had this apogee of verbal expression come from? It was that funny little island once again.

For the life of her and her sister, the global influence, for good and for bad, which this tiny little place had had on the development of humanity, was truly confounding. It was not that there had not been plenty of larger competitors out there who had tried, with varying degrees of success, to foist themselves and their credos on the rest of the planet. But this lot had managed to occupy and influence most of it in recent times. In doing so they had, by times, probably been responsible for more grief and sadness, and slavery and Death, than anyone else, even the religions. That notwithstanding, they had also been a nexus for much of the creativity and development that had evolved side by side with the increasing violence and carnage that was occurring upon her sister. Luna had even gone so far as to think that of all the nations that humanity had divided itself into, it was this odd little island that was the most emblematic of the bewildering dichotomies that these apes presented.

Of late, however, whatever star that was shining on this tiny and odd-shaped little place, seemed to be on the wane. In standing for a good time alone against the genocidal evil that had lately manifested, it had taken a hell of a battering. The apes there had shown themselves to be courageous and unrelenting in their fight against the evil, but they were shattered and broken by the time the war had come to a conclusion.

Would this strange little place ever rise again? It seemed unlikely. Yes, they would go on, but, it seemed to the little moon, just as had happened with every great human empire that had ever existed, it would soon succumb to the rise of new powers and slowly recede back into the anonymity from whence long ago it had come, to leave behind but a history, and a language.

Ordinarily, so the two guardians of Life had noticed, languages receded and often died with the civilisation and empires that had carried them to prominence. At best they might hang on in the countries of their origin, in some of the dominions over which those empires had once extended, or become the objects of academic study and the reserve of but a few. But English, as it was named, after one part of the strange little place, seemed determined to be different in this respect. It had taken on a Life of its own and was increasingly being spoken everywhere, even outside the considerable boundaries of the now fading empire with which it was associated. Nevertheless, as with the people who had given rise to it, this language vied in an increasingly successful manner for supremacy in the worlds of trade and business, and science and technology as, ironically, the 'lingua franca'. The empire was receding at a great rate, and within a few handfuls of cycles would hardly exist at all; but the language refused to die and, indeed, prospered.

Gaia, for her part, was absolutely livid at these latest detonations, and her demeanour got rapidly worse. Though the global conflagration had been ended by the advent of this new weapon, and the apes had started the process of rebuilding once more, they did not stop exploding these massive and terrible devices. Not a moment seemed to go by now without one of the damned things being let off somewhere on her surface. For her it was like going back in time to some of her earliest and most difficult memories when, amidst the organised chaos of his creation, the will of the G had declared that everyone in the vicinity be constantly peppered by the various species of astral ne'er do wells. Back then, they had weathered that stormy period together, but now it was from upon Gaia alone that increasingly large explosions were cratering her surface and destroying vast remote eco systems as they did so; and Luna could but helplessly look on whilst trying to shake the dark images of the 'thin people' from her mind.

As the little island receded in influence, the new powers that had arisen from the ashes of the last war were now honing and refining their newfound mastery of the atom at a hell of a pace. They raced each other to see who might possess the largest arsenal of these ever more powerful weapons. They even gave a new name to this insane rush toward guaranteed self-obliteration, if ever anyone used them in earnest; the 'Cold War'.

That denomination seemed almost as much of a laughable oxymoron as had the invention of the epithet 'sapiens' had a few centuries before. There was nothing cold about it as far Gaia and Luna could see. The scientists and technologists had rapidly gone beyond harnessing the power of splitting atoms to employ the very processes by which the Sun blessed them all with his radiance. Those elemental forces, which had conspired with Gaia and Luna, under the ever-present grace of the G, to yield the benediction that was Gaia's Life, were now being co-opted by the humans to the task of creating levels of destruction the likes of which Gaia had experienced only at the behest of the largest asteroids, meteorites, and the comets who been impelled to end their existence with her. What was more, these new weapons brought with them an entirely new type of fear and paranoia within the apes. As far as Luna was concerned, the first acts of a globalised humanity were warfare, and the creation of a fear the likes of which has never previously been known.

It had to be said, however, that from that point on, there were no more world-encompassing conflicts of the likes that they had recently witnessed, though this was not to say that the prosecution of war had ceased. Around the globe, conflict persisted just as it had always done in the hominid world, and was now often sponsored, in what Gaia and Luna both thought a terribly dishonourable and cowardly way, by the two main rivals for global supremacy that had emerged from the second of the world wars. Such were the arsenals of destruction they now possessed, more than enough to ensure mutual obliteration, they dared not confront each other directly. Instead, they preferred to incite conflict and spread Death amongst others of their kind elsewhere around the globe. More than once they came to the brink of what would have been truly terrible, possibly mass-extinction level conflicts, but in the end, somehow, they did not.

At the same time, and largely as a result of all the time and effort they had been putting into creating these new weapons, and the methods required to deliver them vast distances, they had started up a new game. Apparently, invading and raping every corner of 'their' planet was no longer enough, and with the launch of a rocket that held within it a tiny metallic capsule destined to circle Gaia for just a short period of time, beeping as it went, they started invading space itself.

Within a few tens of cycles, and set against a backdrop of the ever more fulgurant explosions of their weapon testing, and their ever-louder broadcasting into the depths of space, they were throwing all sorts of stuff up around Gaia, Luna, and the other residents of the vicinity, with the inevitable consequences.

Venus became even more shrill, abusive, and deranged than ever, cackling and whooping madly as her atmosphere incinerated the projectiles that that apes aimed at her. Even Mercury was targeted, as was Mars, and eventually, the outer planets. Whilst Luna and Gaia, and indeed Mars, understood that these later happenings owed more to an innate curiosity and a desire to learn, than to the much darker and destructive obsessions of the hominids, it seemed to them that what had been for so long a wonderful place to be, was now becoming an ever more trying, noisy, and downright messy, part of the cosmos. Not content with abusing all that Gaia provided for them, not to say each other, they now seemed to want to pollute space itself.

It was not all bad news, however, and amidst all the burgeoning chaos of Life, Luna, who by now was really in need of a fillip, could not but help note some encouraging signs. For some time now she had observed that, in spite of all the fighting and death and despoiling, there seemed to be undercurrents of change that were rising amongst the humans. Increasingly, and over significant portions of her sister, individuals and societies were rising up to stand against many of the more asinine propositions of those who governed, and which had long time been regarded as simply how things were. Beneath the constant tumult of warfare and strife that had so enveloped Gaia over the last couple of centuries, more and more of the hominids had become educated and, as a result, had then decided to reject what had previously been foisted upon them and demand new ways of doing things.

New thinkers and thinking had arisen amidst the chaos to challenge the precepts of centuries. New scientific discoveries continued to lay bare the absurdity of many a proposition, and to shake many religions, together with their hypocritical adherents, to their very foundations. Established orders were challenged with ever-greater ardour, and some even dared to proclaim that god was dead. By contrast, Luna noted, that the 'big G' only gained in their estimation and, as their scientific understanding increased, was being re-branded by the apes within a new concept called 'space-time', not that that mattered at all to any of the inhabitants of their little system, as it only reaffirmed, and further added to, the magnificence of the G.

Around much of the world the abhorrence of slavery had been seen for the terrible and shameful thing it was and had been abandoned. The enmities that had been nourished by the perverse ideologies that persecuted people according to the colour of their skin, or their sexuality, were being seen for what they were, and were being eradicated, albeit at painfully slow rate. The females were rising up against their oppressors and were gradually reclaiming the rights that had so long been denied them. More and more a clamour could be heard against the madness of warfare, and the seeking of better ways to share the planet with other hominids and all the inhabitants of Gaia's surface who had been so disgracefully treated. They had even, of late, decided to end the mass slaughter of the whales, and those cetaceans that had survived the onslaught over the centuries would now, by and large, be left in some sort of peace to go about their business. It was only a relative peace, however, as even their previously tranquil world was no longer such. As with everywhere else, the apes insisted in spreading their mess and noise into even this tenebrous domain.

All this notwithstanding, Luna had also observed a decided change in both herself and her sister. Luna was still harried by the images of the 'thin people', and by what all the meteoric explosions and industrial pollution were doing to Gaia. For her part Gaia said little, but she did not have to, such was the understanding that existed between the two of them as they danced eternally around the Sun. Luna could feel that there was something wrong. She sensed in her sister an anger, one that had been growing latently for centuries, and that was rapidly crystallising into a rage.

"How dare they! Those stupid little bastards!" Gaia finally exhorted, at last unable to contain herself, the anger just too much. She even found a moment to dispense such vitriolic tirade of abuse at the constantly carping Venus that the latter promptly shut up and sloped off.

Luna, for her part, was shocked once more at Gaia's descent into what she now regarded as a very 'human' way to behave. Somewhat inexplicably, however, she found herself enthusiastically joining in with the expletive ridden stream of invective that her sister deployed. As brief as it was, when it was over and Venus had been sent packing in no uncertain terms, Luna could find no consolation in what they had just done. If anything, upon recalling the tragic events that had overtaken Venus long ago, she felt even worse and went the colour of Mars for a bit, something, that was for her, a rare event.

Mars, who had heard everything as he hoved into the vicinity, gently asked what was up?

"Oh!" exclaimed Gaia. "It's my Life… I'm just so fed up with it, I hate my Life!" starting to sob uncontrollably as she did so.

Luna was aghast, she had never seen her sister in such a state, not even way back when she was perpetually convulsed by forces the power of which were immense, even compared to what had lately transpired.

"No, no, no!" she interjected. "It's not your Life, it's just those bloody monkeys, everything else is beautiful and balanced and sustainable."

"They're not monkeys, they're apes!" Gaia wailed back.

"Oh! Whatever!" Luna abruptly retorted before continuing. "What matters is what they are doing to you. They're ruining everything, the little shits! What the fuck is wrong with them! You spend all your time looking after them, looking over them, caring for them, and how do they repay you? They dig great big holes in you, then burn stuff, and put all sorts of shit all over you. They rape and despoil anything they come into contact with, think only about themselves, and forget about you to the point that they start acting like asteroids or meteorites!"

"Oh Luna! Where did we go wrong?" Gaia sobbed. "Not so long ago, they were our darlings, but look at them now. Spoilt, greedy little creatures who have the capacity to destroy not only themselves but also everything else around them. They're… they're…" She stammered, as she struggled to come up with something adequate, only to suddenly blurt out, "Ooooh, we've made terror-formers! That's what they are, terror-formers! Oh, I am so ashamed!" she finally exclaimed, before collapsing into more terrible sobbing.

Luna did not know what to say, and could but look imploringly at Mars, who seemed to be even redder than usual, stunned as he was by the language and sentiments that had suddenly burst forth from his two friends.

"Well, why don't you just get rid of them then?" the red planet eventually suggested, as gently as he could. "You know, start afresh? From what I can now see they do seem rather delinquent, and not a bit dim. My G, they associate me with war, Venus with love, think Saturn is a bloke, and as to Panic and Fear here," at this he indicated his two moons as they whizzed about him. "I mean: how ridiculous is that! And all this awful noise and throwing things about the place! Might we not all be better off without them?"

A moment passed before, choking back her sobs, Gaia replied, "You know. I have considered it. Getting rid of them I mean."

Luna felt a shudder run from her core to all points on her surface as Gaia's anger and distress suddenly seemed to morph into something far colder and decidedly menacing. She said nothing immediately, so stunned was she. But in no more than the time it took her to complete a couple of rotations around her sister, Luna then timidly admitted to her companions the dark nature of the thoughts that, for a hundred or so cycles, had so plagued her.

In response, Gaia simply shifted the clouds that were swirling over one of the continents of her northern hemisphere, in such a graceful and delicate manner, that her compassion toward her sister was instantaneously conveyed, and even Mars seemed moved.

"But I have decided, that it would be wrong to do so," Gaia finally stated, suddenly mastering her emotions.

"I mean, I feel I have it within me, an extinction-level event I mean. There are certain parts of me that, if I concentrated really hard, I could make explode with such violence that I would blacken myself for a hundred cycles. More than enough to finish them off, I think. For all their clever ways and their technology, just look at them! They are not so robust. There is a frailty to them that their own self-importance belies. Perhaps that is even part the reason that they are like they are? That deep down they know this, but are just too afraid to admit it; and instead they distract themselves from this truth with all this pointless aggression and consumption and noise and mess.

She paused, before continuing.

"However, and although I am no expert in celestial ethics, everything I feel, right to my molten core, says that whatever happens we have been blessed, and that it is our duty to give them, and Life in general, its chance, and to allow it to take the direction that it has to take. I mean, look at poor Venus and what happened to her. She could do nothing about that, it was just the will of the G. When I think of her, and what we recently did to her, an act that I am not at all proud of, I come to the conclusion that we cannot intercede. That we must allow this Life, however troublesome some aspects of it are, to have the right to determine its own destiny. If the G wills otherwise, as he did with those giant reptiles and their like but a little while ago, then we must obey. But no matter what we think or feel, or what transpires next, we must remain dispassionate, and act only as observers and recorders."

And there she stopped, her little soliloquy seeming to have calmed her down somewhat, though the odd sniffle persisted. Luna and Mars could but look on and simultaneously think that this was perhaps the noblest thing that they had ever heard; and even if, for his part, Mars would have really appreciated some of the peace and quiet that of late he, along with everyone else, had been so rudely deprived of. He slowly drifted off, taking his boys with him, leaving Luna to look over her sister.

Straight away, and pushing all her unwanted thoughts and feelings in to the background as best she could, Luna decided that a thorough check-up was in order. And in spite of Gaia's protestations that she was fine, that Life had just been a bit stressful of late, and that she was just a bit run down, set about this new task with all the determination that she had displayed ever since Life had appeared beneath her. What with all the recent terrestrial turmoil, it had been a good while since Luna had made a thorough inventory of things and given Gaia a good look over.

And whilst Luna assiduously began thinking about how best to go about this new business, they both became aware that down below she had suddenly become the focus of a great deal of attention amongst the upright apes. The two greatest powers in the hominid world, the ones who had raced each other to arm themselves to the teeth with the most destructive weapons ever created, had taken into their heads to shoot some of their kind into space, and onto her; and all seemingly just to prove who was the greater power!

And, soon enough, the day arrived where virtually all of the ape's attention, not to mention their noisy emissions, lay with Luna and the landing of men upon her. For once, the hominid world stood still as one of their number jumped onto Luna surface for the first time; and the apes appeared to share in a unified elation at this astonishing achievement.

For her part, at any point in time since Life had begun in Gaia's oceans, Luna would have been ecstatic at the thought of actually experiencing Life first-hand; to know, if just for a moment, what it was like to have something alive upon you. But what with all that had transpired recently, and the growing concern she had for her sister's health, she found that she could summon no joy in the 'event' of the hominid's twentieth century AD, as they referred to the current era. On the contrary, given what had been going on down on Gaia's surface recently, apprehension, and not a little anxiety were the only feelings she could only muster. That was until she realised that they were just going to wander around a bit, collect a few rocks, plant one of their flags, and then go away again.

When the day finally came, the event was accompanied, as appeared requisite for the apes, by a proclamation of dubious veracity, and not a little pomposity, as she understood these things, and she paid it little attention. In the end, the whole affair, whilst captivating the hominid world below, passed for her as but a rather mundane and infinitesimal instant. Luna did find some solace in that she had somehow, and if albeit for but a fleeting moment in time, had the power to unite the human race. But the solace, however welcome, was as transitory as the event itself. They came a few times after that, the great powers of the time from the east and from the west of Gaia's northern hemisphere, but then seemed to lose interest in her.

And so she told her sister to take a rest from Life for a bit and got on with her work, which turned out to be the most demanding thing she had ever done. She had always relied on Gaia to tell her about what was going on, what sort of state she was in, what she was feeling, and how she was. However, as she now considered Gaia as a patient of sorts, and whilst she had no reason to doubt the honesty of her sister, nor her own intuition, she felt that this investigation required a different, more objective and analytical approach, much like the scientist apes had developed in the recent centuries. But how was she to achieve such an end?

For a while, the moon was stumped as she circled her sister. After all, there were limits to what she could divine for herself from her tribune in space. But, as with every challenge that Life and its curation had thrown at her — from the progressive adaptation from geological timescales to those of seconds; to the learning of new languages; modes of expression; not to mention entirely new concepts of existence and thought — the diminutive, but tenacious, satellite found a solution; a solution that the hominids themselves provided.

For decades now, they had been chucking stuff up into space. Some of the stuff whizzed out in the direction of her, wheeled about her for a bit, and then died. Some of it was directed at Venus, Mars, and latterly toward the outer planets and the Sun. But having done whatever it was meant to do, it then also died. Most of the stuff, however, went up to orbit Gaia, and appeared to be designed to stay there for a good while; and within a very short time there were hundreds of these things whirling about her sister.

Right from the first incursion of the funny little beeping sphere into space, Gaia and Luna had puzzled over what was the purpose of these things. They had initially thought that this was just another manifestation of the national and political one-upmanship that so seemed to obsess the 'sapiens', albeit a decidedly more serene expression of it than the wars or the weapons testing. But they soon realised that there was much more to these funny little objects that were, with ever greater frequency and complexity to their design, being hurled into space around Gaia.

As Luna studied them, and the emissions from Gaia that were now part of every second of her existence, she realised that some of the smarter apes had understood that hurling their technology into space could provide all sorts of new means of communicating, and/or gathering information about each other, herself, Gaia, and the cosmos in general. They had even understood how to make some of these things stay in orbit over certain parts of Gaia rather than just fly round and about her. As she learned more about this celestial clutter, and what most of it was designed for, Luna found herself warming once more, if only just a little, to this most troublesome and potentially dangerous emanation of Life. They were indeed very clever, and amidst all the stupidity they had demonstrated there was still a glimmer of hope, she thought.

Some these things, she rapidly understood, could provide the objective analysis that her new task required. And so she set herself to decoding the signals that these objects received and the emissions they made, even if they were often highly directional and difficult to find amidst the maelstrom of electromagnetic noise that was now heading her way. They also chuntered away at speeds that were so rapid that, once again, she had to alter her own concept of time and concentrate as never before to keep up with them.

But, little by little, and cycle by cycle around her sister, she managed to grasp some of the new languages by which these tiny, fast-moving, chunks of metal were controlled and, more importantly, what they were saying. As she did so, she realised that, as usual, a lot of these things had been put place by various governments and their militaries to spy on one another, or to direct their engines of war to whatever poor place was to be the recipient of their benediction; a fact that depressed her no end. Then there were the satellites, as the apes called them, that were charged with communications and spreading the endless streams of chatter and images that the apes appeared increasingly addicted to; and whilst she found some of these things intriguing, not to say sometimes informative, beautiful, or downright funny, she passed those over as well as they were not what she required. Instead, she homed in on those objects that were concerned with more scientific assessments of Gaia, of which there were a growing profusion, and concentrated on them.

The result, as the cycles wore on and the ape tech got more and more advanced, was that she experienced what she could only describe as a 'dataclasm'. Such was the torrent of information that these things were producing that, for the first time since Life had appeared, Luna found she could not cope; it was just all too much. More than that, as the technology advanced, the languages that these satellites used became more complex, dense, and difficult to decipher.

Luna realised that she had reached a point where keeping up with all this data was beyond her, and that she needed help. But from whom could she ask it? Venus was out of the question, and so once again, as Mars and his boys rounded into their closest approach to Gaia, she hailed him and explained the problem.

As it happened, Mars had just been paid a visit by a couple of little machines that were still circling him, and which had dropped a couple of other little machines onto his surface to have a look around and a poke about. Fortunately, Mars was of a calm disposition and, as a result of monitoring their emissions, had prepared for this invasion of his space, even joking that, given his colour, how could he be anything but sanguine!

More than that, however, Luna was then both surprised and happy to hear that, not only was Mars up to date as to the nature and seriousness or her endeavour, but that he even had a plan of action.

"My boys, and Eureka and her gang, will not let you down," he stated quite categorically, before adding that they too had been observing the situation, and were more than happy to help out in any way that they could.

Luna was overtaken by a feeling of relief and at this news, as she really was in terrible fix. Such was the growing profusion of these objects and the information they were relaying that needed to be decoded and analysed, not to mention all the other detritus that perpetually peppered her senses, that she was overrun.

"See my boy Panic here?" Mars continued, chuckling as he did so at the thought of this ridiculous hominid nomenclature, "Well, he may be a bit on the small side, and rather a strange shape, and to be honest, most of what he does say I do not understand, but he's a whizz with codes and maths and the like. I would hazard that he can you into anywhere given a bit of time and study. And as for analysis, you will not find a finer mind hereabouts. But everything," — and once more he giggled to himself — "has to go through Fear here, or Eureka over there, as they're the only ones who can understand what he says. You tell us where to look, and we'll take care of the rest; and whatever we can't handle, we can farm out to the gassers and their tribes."

Luna could not help but blush just a little, overwhelmed as she was by this entirely unexpected pronouncement and the compassion that Mars and his little band had for their situation. Gaia too, as she could not but overhear what was going on, joined in and thanked them all for their wonderful amity. She added, however, that she thought it best that they should keep this to themselves, at least for the moment. Jupiter had, of late, seemed not at all well disposed toward Gaia's apes, given all the noise and the mess that had recently appeared. She did not think it wise, therefore, to bother him, or anyone else on the other side of the asteroid belt, at least for now.

Mars ruminated on this last observation and then conceded that maybe Gaia had a point, before he and his little collective went on their way charged with their new mission.

Luna immediately indicated to them where to look, and in what parts of the electromagnetic spectrum, as soon as she identified a potential new source of information, or one that she had already tagged but had not been able to access or comprehend completely; and then Mars and his boys, aided and abetted by the tiny Eureka and her strange little clan, got to work.

Not that this was easy for them, being so much further away. They had to learn to work as a team as they had never had to do before and, just like Luna, had to train themselves to keep pace with the extreme speed of the emissions once they had located them. Mars acted as the seeker and as the primary information buffer, grabbing as much information as he could once the target emissions had been identified. In parallel he relayed the information to Fear and Eureka, who then translated it into the curious language that they and the oblate Panic used to communicate with each other; and then Panic got stuck in.

It transpired that Mars had not been understating the capacities of his tiny and oddly shaped moon. The little fellow was indeed some sort of strange genius, who in spite of his looks and his incomprehensible parole, rapidly made mincemeat of any signals, however complex, that came his way. If anything, he was too fast, and it was Mars, Fear, and Eureka who found themselves straining under the bi-directional deluge of information that they had to deal with, especially as Panic was not given to direct and literal explanations. He seemed to see the universe in a particularly prosaic way that caused no end of challenges to interpretation.

"What a time for little bugger to decide he is a poet!" Mars jovially exclaimed, whilst inadvertently revealing that he too seemed to have been struck by the curious charm of profanity, in the middle a particularly difficult and extended data dump with Luna.

"But isn't he brilliant, you must be so proud!" Luna exclaimed, ecstatic at their progress, and even if she was run of her axis.

"I mean..." she hesitated, "no offence intended, but I would never have thought!"

"None taken!" Mars boomed back "This is the best thing that has ever happened to him, his brother, and Eureka and her little band of rogues! They're having so much fun! I wish, in many ways, that the circumstances were different, but really I should be thanking you. And if nothing else, none of them have recently bothered tuning into any of those other broadcasts that so fill the aether these days... I mean, have you seen some of it? Anyway, have to go. We have a lot more to get through yet, and it seems they have just launched another probe. To go visit Jupiter! I can just imagine what he will think of that, so best be prepared!"

And with that, the Martians once again wheeled off, leaving Luna to continue her studies.

Luna, of course, had seen all too much of the emissions Mars was referring to, and it was only with extreme concentration that she was able to filter out all the distractive nonsense that now incessantly emanated from Gaia. Indeed, of late she had really tried not to look down at all, and had instructed Gaia not to tell her anything unless it was really urgent.

She had to admit, however, that to call all of it nonsense was overstating the case. For a start, there was that wondrous and diverse thing called music that everyone seemed to appreciate. Beyond that, there was also a great deal that was to be admired, and that was of real interest to her intellectual and socio-psychological sides, in much that came her way. It was true to say, however, that these nuggets had to be sieved from within the ever-growing morass of inanity that the apes seemed hell bent on creating, and then spreading willy-nilly into the neighbourhood.

But right now, she could not afford the luxury of such distractions, even the music; and anyway, she had learned that the stuff that she was really interested in would more than likely be repeated well into the future, and that she could catch up with it somewhen.

There were other things, however, that she desperately tried to keep out, as if she caught a glimpse of them she would be immediately transported back to those horrifying events of but a few decades ago.

The 'thin people' had not left her, and still lurked in the recesses of her mind. And, in spite of her trying to screen as much as she could, her mental defences and discipline had, on occasion, failed her recently; and when they did more unwanted and disturbing images flooded in. Most of these she could rapidly deal with and shut out, but recently, and on more than one occasion, she had been assailed by more images of large numbers of thin and dying, or dead, hominids.

On a seemingly regular basis during this period, famine and pestilence assailed parts of the human race to add to the misery of many of the apes. Famine and pestilence had, of course, always been there, occasionally rearing their ugly heads to decimate populations of all sorts of species all over her sister's surface. In the past, Luna had thought of them simply as an integral part of the balancing act that was Life, just as the mass extinctions caused by external interlopers were just part of how the cosmos worked.

Lately, however, and as and when some of these things has slipped through her defences, she had seen a great many 'thin people' in various places. Somehow, however, whilst emaciated, and often either dead or very close to Death, these 'thin people' seemed different to the ones that had manifested toward the end of the apes' second great global war. These ones, whilst generally very thin from starvation, often also bore with them the distended abdomens that were indicative of malnutrition, as well. And in their eyes, and specifically the eyes of the children, Life seemed far from expunged. Instead, the Life that remained within them seemed to be pleading with her to be allowed to continue. As a result, Luna could not say whether they, and the reasons for their existence, were even more disturbing than those who had gone before.

And whereas beforehand the 'thin people' had appeared as a result of some sort of insane vindictiveness on the part of a small number of apes who, for reasons that still eluded her, had tried to annihilate a single, ethnic grouping, now they were appearing in a lot of different places. Moreover, what afflicted them seemed to have no preference for their creed or ethnicity, save for that none of the afflicted appeared to be what the humans referred to as 'white'.

Aside from being uniformly upsetting, Luna puzzled over why this was happening. Was it simply the result of and increased coverage of such things by the apes and their now extensive communications networks? Or, was this evidence of the human world going wrong in a variety of other ways. These events could hardly be squared with the astounding leaps that they had made as a species in all forms of science and technology, nor the relative luxury and wealth of many countries? Were these poor innocents, therefore, a by-product of the incessant feuding between the two dominant ideologies of the times; collateral damage that resulted from their cowardly wars fought by proxy? Or were they simply deemed an acceptable side-effect of the increasingly rapacious and greedy economic systems of the wealthy west, which appeared not to value anything but money, and therefore had scant regard for anything else?

That said, she also saw that an awful lot of people in the 'developed world' were not anywhere near as selfish, greedy, and nasty as some of their systems appeared to be, and did try their level best to ameliorate the terrible famines as they could. But it was not, by and large, the religions, or governments, or the rich, or the corporations, who, for the most part, lead the way in this respect. Some organisations within these factions did try to provide aid to these poor people, but astonishingly at this time the biggest and most effective reaction to these terrible situations seemed come from musicians and other artists led by a charismatic Irish ape called Bob. It was Bob and his friends, not the governments and organisations that wielded most of the power, who appeared to force the required issues and, with the help of many millions of ordinary folk, managed to do a great deal of good.

And in this Luna once more found some consolation. They were not all greedy and selfish. But she still could not understand why all these good people did not think about changing the way things were done? It was not, in general, the people, but the horrible, avaricious, and relentless political and economic systems that were being collectively insisted upon, which seemed to be the ultimate source of the great many of the problems that afflicted the apes and her sister. And no matter how good many of the apes might have shown themselves to be, were they not still, if not consciously, complicit with these systems and, therefore, the very sources of all these terrible things?

Whatever the case, and whilst she was not proud of it, she could not afford to think about these things, and with a heavy core she shut them out as best she could. The health of her sister, and finding out what sort of damage the beastly hominids might be doing to her, had to remain her priority.

A couple of decades or so later, in one of his regular reports back to Luna, Mars, still chuckling at the ridiculous ape-isms by which they knew his moons, announced that 'his boy Panic' had come up with another way to gather the sorts of data that Luna needed; one that might be considerably more efficient than the manner they had been harvesting information up to now.

"Another way? What's that?" replied Luna, at once very interested in anything that would help her better understand what was going on down below, but equally a little tremulous at the thought of even more data to deal with.

"Well," he began in characteristic manner, and appearing very proud indeed, "it seems that Panic here was finding all this code cracking and stuff too easy for him, and he was getting a bit bored. And so, on the side, he started following the information to see if he could work out where it was going and what the apes were doing with it."

"Oh my!" Luna thought, suddenly eager to hear more. "And what has he found?"

"A treasure trove, my dear! A veritable treasure trove! What he has found is that for some time now those scientific types have been recording and collating all sorts of data, much like you and Gaia have done over the eons. And…" he continued, "they have developed all sorts of ways of seeing back into the past, working out how things were, and how they changed thousands and thousands of cycles ago. What's more the level of detail that they can now achieve is quite remarkable; and as they have started digitising everything, Panic here can read it. And that means we now have access to it all as well!"

At this he started cackling to himself and was immediately joined by both his charges before he carried on.

"It even appears that some of them down there are doing exactly what we are doing. They too, and a growing number it would seem, are also very concerned about how things are going. And guess what! One of them has even remembered Gaia's name!"

"Really!" Luna replied; it had been a long time since anyone down below had actually called her by name.

"But this is wonderful news, Mars! How can we thank you all? How soon can we have this new information uploaded, do you think?"

"Soon as you like," he stated laconically "But there is so, so much more. The little blighter hasn't stopped there."

At this he suddenly paused, and his demeanour and expression took on a decidedly conspiratorial aspect.

"He has gone much, much, further." Now Mars was whispering, much to the surprise, not to say amusement, of both Gaia and Luna. "He has hacked his way into their military and governmental systems. The Pentagon, the Kremlin, the CIA, MI5, MI6, the KGB, Mossad, Beijing, the big corporations too... You name it... Oh, if you could know what we have come to know lately. My G! But, very revealing, and sometimes decidedly concerning as that stuff is, it is for another time I feel, and not immediately a propos to the matters to hand."

And with that he stopped, and they all paused for a moment, to ponder what Mars had just revealed. Of course, Gaia and Luna knew of all the places and organisations that he had just mentioned; how could they not with the ceaseless barrage of emissions, fictional or otherwise, that were ejected their way. But, much as they both found themselves insatiably curious about what the Martians had lately discovered, they could but agree that would have to wait for another, quieter time. More than that, however, Luna sensed an opportunity amidst the great pride Mars was expressing in respect of his moons and their new found status of keepers of all the secrets that the apes guarded most closely.

"I do have another favour to ask of you, if I may," she therefore immediately added.

"Of course my dear, fire away!" came back the enthusiastic reply she had hoped for.

"Well…" She hesitated. "I was wondering." She hesitated again, not knowing quite how to proceed.

"Come on, out with it!" Mars boomed back, still apparently joyous in his new role.

"Well…" she repeated, pausing slightly before rattling out as fast as she could,

"I was wondering whether you could have a word with Venus and find out as much as you can about what happened to her? I mean, not all of it, but the details of how it started, what were the symptoms, how things progressed, and at what point it all became unstoppable and irreversible."

"Please," she then added with as much charm as she could muster, knowing full well what she was asking.

All of a sudden, Mars's northerly cap seemed to droop, and his canals sag, at the rattled-out request. If there had ever been such ever a planetary expression of foreboding, the countenance of Mars had suddenly descended into it. For a split second even his boys also seemed to stop still about him in utter astonishment, whining in simultaneous disapproval as they did so.

"Oh!" he sighed after a long moment of reflection amidst the waves of electromagnetic detritus that was barrelling out in all directions from Gaia, "Well, I cannot say that what you have just asked me to do fills me with glee. It does not."

At this he paused, whilst seeming to glow in a manner that Luna and Gaia had not previously observed, before stating, "But I shall try."

And with that, off they popped again, intercepting data streams, and decoding and translating as they went.

"Did you see that?" Gaia asked Luna.

"Yes, I did. I've never seen Mars go that colour before, what do you think it might mean?" Luna replied.

"You know, I'm really not sure." Came the reply, before she added quickly and sharply, "And I'm not a bloody hypothesis!"

To this Luna did not respond, as she did not understand whether her sister was having a little joke, regarding the apparent remembrance of her name by at least one out of the many billion hominids that now swarmed over her, or might have be genuinely upset by this new epithet?

Cycles, different for all of them, spun by. Satellite communications were hacked, information sped back and forth about the inner solar system, and the business of assessing Gaia's state, and what the hominids were doing to her, went on. Amidst all of the extra-terrestrial activity, the apes too went about their business, blissfully unaware that they were now the object of study, analysis, and contemplation. The insignificant little system, which the G had bequeathed to this part of his giant creation, was now fully occupied and agog at the confounding nature, and contradictory qualities, of the strange beings that had sprung up amongst them upon the third stone from their Sun.

In the meantime, one of the objects that the apes had launched into the solar system, the one that years ago had been aimed at Jupiter, had managed to leave it for the depths of deep space. For his part, Jupiter had seemed not so bothered by this sort of intrusion; it was the noise he could not abide. He had let it slip, however, that he did not like the way these apes had contrived to use him to sling-shot the damnable thing to go and bother others; it seemed rather disrespectful, to say the least, in his opinion.

Indeed, all the wanderers had been, or were soon to be paid, visits by the little machines that the apes kept throwing at them. On one occasion, even the unflappable Mars got himself into a bit of a state when bam! One of these little things didn't stop and careered into him as if it were a meteorite.

"What the fuck!" he was heard to exclaim, confirming that he too appeared have come under the influence of this remarkable profanity, and for just a short time he was as angry as anyone could remember him being. That was, until they understood why this had happened. Far from being some act of aggression or war, it turned out that some of the very cleverest of the sapiens had contrived to mix up two different systems of measurement; specifically, two measurements of distance. The result was that this little machine thought it still had some way to go before it reached Mars and simply failed to stop! When, via Fear, Panic explained this, Mars's anger instantly transformed into an incontrollable laughter that lasted for a good few cycles, and which slowed down the process of data theft no end for a while.

Not long after that, Jupiter then had the opportunity to demonstrate just how important and powerful he was, by taking one for the team in the shape of a comet that had he subtly coerced into ending itself with him.

From time to time, over the eons of their existence, Jupiter's mass could not help but attract all sorts of flotsam and jetsam into his orbit, doing everyone else a big favour in the process; and, having enticed them in, he would sometimes take his time to play with them a bit before finally consuming them. This side of Jupiter left the inner planets a little uneasy, much as they were all happy that these invaders from G knows where had been drawn to him rather than into them. But, as they would all look on whenever such an event had commenced, they sometimes got the impression that the great gas giant took just a little too much pleasure in conducting these little dances of destruction toward their inevitable conclusion. This time, however, and for the first time, they were not the only onlookers. The apes too were observing events with their satellites and their telescopes, one of which, a really big one, they had recently managed to throw in orbit around Gaia, just to add to the clutter.

If nothing else, Jupiter proved himself to be quite the showman and, possibly egged on by the knowledge that he had a new audience, he took his time with this comet. He hooked it, and then drew it in. He even allowed it to orbit him for a while before his implacable gravity crushed it in to bits; pieces that, if they had flown into Gaia or Luna or Mars, could still have done some serious damage. But he was not done there. He then strung the bits out, as if expressly for his new Gaian audience, into a line that eventually he permitted to career into him and to be disintegrated under his irresistible power, leaving his outer atmosphere in visible disarray for some time.

"'Tis but a flesh wound!" he then loudly proclaimed, before bursting into hearty guffaws, much to the amusement of everyone else. And, as the last of the comet disappeared into the vast swirls of his outer self, the signals that they were all now monitoring told them that Jupiter had at last achieved the sort of stardom, albeit transiently, that he had so long ago been denied by the G; and they could hardly begrudge him that.

A little while later, however, one of the hominids' other deep space probes caused an absolute commotion amongst the wanderers. This was a satellite that had flown by Venus, Gaia, and Jupiter, in its efforts to get to Saturn, whom it was destined to study for as long as it could. All along the way it recorded things and took pictures, which nobody seemed to mind at all. They also knew that it carried another little machine which the humans wanted to deposit upon Titan, the largest of Saturn's moons, to find out more about him; and nobody seemed to mind about that either. That was until it actually landed, and the previously rather smug Titan, who ever since they had all found out about it had boasted to all and sundry about how special he must be have been chosen by the apes to be the first moon outside of Luna to be landed upon, had a panic attack!

"Aaargh! Get it off me! Get it off me! Help! Help! I can feel it contaminating me!" he was suddenly heard to shriek and wail, spreading panic amongst Saturn's large clan of orbiters. Needless to say, Saturn was not at all amused, and her normally calm and demure comportment evaporated completely. She did not go so far as to utter any of the profanities that had latterly spread like a virus throughout the system, but she lambasted Jupiter for not having contrived to do anything about the passage of this object, not seeming to understand that not even the great Jove could do anything at all about it.

Jupiter responded in kind. Titan, he retorted, was just behaving like 'a big baby', and all of a sudden, a great argument broke out between the gas giants and their gaggles. Mars did his best to calm the situation, pointing out that none of them had any agency in respect of the apes and their machines, and that both he and Luna had been landed upon plenty of times, and nothing bad had come of it. But his diplomatic efforts came to no avail.

What latterly became known throughout the system as the 'Huyghens incident' raged until the point when both Luna and Gaia could no longer stand it and stepped in to plead with them all to stop and think about what they were doing. They had all started behaving like some of the hominids! The scientist apes and their little machines meant no harm; they were just curious about them all, and Titan would be fine.

This intervention did at least have the desired effect in calming everyone down, though for a good while relations between the two gas giants and their clans, not to mention between them and the hard bodies that existed on the other side of the asteroid belt, were less than cordial.

"What about all the bloody noise?" was Jupiter's closing remark, as he always had to have the last word. To that issue, neither Gaia nor Luna could muster an answer. In that respect, the extinction of the human race or, possibly, the collapse of their civilisations into a much less technologically advanced state, seemed to be the only currently available solutions. But Gaia reaffirmed her position that she would not interfere with her Life. Only the almighty G was in possession of such a remit. And as devoted adherents of the G, Jupiter and Saturn could but concede on that point.

Time went on, and after a further decade and a half of monitoring, analysing, and cross-referencing, and not a little into the new century (according to the hominids' latest system of dating things), Luna had seen and had enough. She was tired, felt inexplicably weak, and was experiencing ever greater difficulties in keeping out the unwanted images and sounds that constantly battered her. And then there was the data that they had all so assiduously harvested, compiled, and then analysed over the years; a quite gargantuan amount of data that to her mind did not bode at all well for her sister's health and immediate future. She therefore summoned the strength to tell Mars that they should stop their data retrieval activities. What they needed to do now was to try and understand precisely what state Gaia was in, and what might happen to her sister, and indeed all the Life she hosted, if the apes kept on doing what they were doing.

Mars assented, but as he and his band came into perigee, he could but exclaim to them both, "Oh my G! Are you all right, my dear? You seem terribly pale. And Gaia! My word, your caps! Well, I sort of knew, obviously, but I hadn't realised the extent! And so quickly!"

"No, Mars, I am far from being OK," Luna sighed. "It's the stress of doing all this, I think. I am just worn out, and Gaia's temperature just keeps on going up, as you say, so quickly. We've never seen anything like this before." At this, Gaia could only muster a sniffled, "Hi Mars," and it was only too evident that she was really not herself.

Mars then went a funny colour again and, stumbling over his words, blurted out, "Yes. OK. I see. We should get going on that as soon as we can..." He paused. "But," he carried on, "I... errrr, have to, go for a quick eclipse just now. You know, as we all have to do from time to time. You know how it is. But fear not, we'll be back in a jiffy and we can sort through all this stuff together."

And with that, he his boys wheeled off in an arc that, it was true, would take then rapidly into solar eclipse.

"Did you see that?" Gaia sniffed.

"Yes I did. That colour again?" Luna sighed back "What's going on with him, do you think?"

"No idea," came the somewhat listless reply from down below.

Luna did not say anything. Carelessly, she had allowed herself to wander back to the current state of her sister, upon whom of late there had been a rash of very large wildfires. From California and Brazil to Australia and even Scandinavia, vast swathes of Gaia's beautiful forests were burning; and all, either directly or indirectly, as a result of the apes and their wanton behaviour.

All of a sudden she felt decidedly queasy. She thought she felt her insides moving about, as she allowed the images of the burning forests to dance their flaming dance within her mind's eye. The vast writhing tongues of the fires were curiously hypnotic and, as she involuntarily allowed them to wash over her, she had the sense that all the knowledge and information she had retained over the eons, all that she had seen from her position on high, was suddenly weighing very heavily upon her in a manner that was decidedly uncomfortable and oppressive.

She tried to concentrate upon the firmament about her, to wrest her mind from these fiery images and uncomfortable sensations, and was surprised to find that there appeared to be fewer stars about her than there normally were. How odd, she thought, before she gathered herself and looked again.

"Oh my G!" she gasped, then, "Gaia! Gaia! Where are the stars going! What's happening? The stars, the stars! They're going out!"

"What are you talking about, sister?" came the response from down below. "Nothing is happening to the stars. Are you alright?"

A brief silence ensued as Luna continued to stare onto the heavens, thinking that she was now shaking uncontrollably, and that something was pressing in on her, as the stars continued to disappear.

"Luna, I said are you all right? Say something please! Look at me, Luna!" Now Gaia could sense something was decidedly wrong as Luna stammered back, her voice now weak and quivering, that the stars were abandoning her, that she was dizzy and couldn't breathe, and that she mustn't look down!

Gaia was nonplussed and immediately anxious, "But what do you mean, sister, we don't breathe? And why shouldn't you look at me? There is nothing to be afraid of. What's up? Look at me, Luna, please! Everything's all right. Luna! Please! Look at me, and you will see everything is fine!"

Luna, her insides seeming now to be vibrating with an alarming frequency, started to panic.

"No sister! I do not think things are fine at all!"

And with her last reserves of strength, Luna looked down to her sister.

Gaia, who for the moment retained her composure, immediately did what she had always done when she thought her little sister was in need of reassurance. She used her atmosphere to conjure up the most soothing flows of white and blue that she could imagine. This time, however, all that happened was that Luna suddenly started shrieking in a terrified, and terrifying, manner.

"Aaargh! What are you doing! What's happening! Stop it! Stop it! Please stop!"

And now it was Gaia's turn to panic, and to cry for help.

What had greeted Luna when she had wrested herself from the apparently disappearing cosmos, was not the image of gently flowing serenity that Gaia was projecting. Instead of her beautiful sister, all bedecked in her blues and whites and greens, she was confronted with a Gaia that was suddenly stippled here and there with what looked like black pustules; hideously shiny buboes that were emanating from Gaia's landmasses. She saw them rise up as welts, before they burst to spew their hideous, black and glutinous contents onto the land. In an instant,

Gaia's continents were inundated, and when the land had been consumed, it continued to spread itself relentlessly over the seas. In no time at all, the vile slick had covered her sister entirely; and all she could hear was her sister's voice pleading for help! And then, to make things worse, Gaia was suddenly enveloped in a halo of red, yellow, and orange flames.

"They're killing her! They're burning and poisoning and killing my sister!" she wailed, as she started to feel a nauseous sensation welling up from deep within herself. She wanted desperately to turn away, but found she could not as something started to manifest within the burning black sphere around which she now orbited.

The hideous black mask began to churn. Whirls of white began to appear and transform what had been her sister into a giant version of that symbol that had, for over a thousand cycles, haunted Luna. And all the time the terrible flaming halo grew in intensity.

"Aaargh!" she screamed again, to punctuate the ever more anguished pleas for help that were coming from what had been her sister.

"A crown of thorns! A flaming crown of thorns!" she wailed. "No! No! don't kill my sister! Please! Please! Take me! Take me! I shall pay for your sins, but please leave my sister be!"

At this, the symbol started to shift again, and to ooze into something even more ghastly; a human skull in whose orbits Death proclaimed itself, before the evil emanation started to cackle.

"Yes! Luna! You will pay! You will pay! Not for our sins, but for yours! And not before you have watched us consume your precious sister and everything that exists upon her! And when we have done that, we shall come for you, and everything else, everywhere, until we have despoiled, blackened, and enslaved the entire cosmos."

"What sins? What have I done? Why do you persecute us so! What is the point of all this!" Luna screamed back at the monstrous entity that was now to be bearing down upon her.

A further hideous cackle thumped into her before the skull retorted, laughing ever more loudly as it did so, "Well! Well! Well! The impertinent little moon requires a justification! Ha ha ha! There is none! Save for our pleasure and our greed, of which there can be no end! And as for your sins, would you like to see, little moon? Do you really not know?"

At this, the skull opened is cavernous black mouth and, one by one, the dead teeth which it contained wobbled, and then fell out to disappear into the unctuous blackness. Now feeling as if she was now about to fall to pieces completely, Luna could but look on, angrily transfixed, as the points into which the teeth had disappeared started to bubble and blister. Then, from each of these points, shapes started to arise and mould themselves into silhouetted forms; forms that Luna began to recognise, and which then proceeded to leach out into the space between her and Gaia.

"No! No!" she screamed, as Luna now saw vast armies of the 'thin people' spew forth toward her. She recognised victims of the famines and the holocaust, who were then followed by the innocent victims of all the genocides, and the wars, and the pestilence that humanity had inflicted upon itself and everything else. Then, from other parts of the hideous mouth, all the slaves manifested, followed in short order by the whales that had been massacred, and then all the other species that the apes had driven to extinction. Lastly, all those countless generations of the Life that had lived, and then respectfully returned themselves to where they had come from, only to be unceremoniously exhumed and burned to drive the ape civilisations as they had spread, rose up as ghastly black smog; an abominable heaving and hateful black mass that now reached out toward the terrified little moon.

"Why are you doing this? Why? Why?" Luna screamed at the apparitions "I did not do this, I didn't do anything! Stop it! Stop it! Stop it! Please!"

But on they came, seeking to surround the screaming satellite, as the skull sneered once more, and shouted triumphantly, "Precisely, little moon! YOU DID NOTHING! You've seen it all, you've watched everything, but YOU DID NOTHING! That, little moon, is your sin; and for that you must now pay!"

The skull then burst into loud contemptuous laughter, as the armies of the dead marched on, spreading out to encircle the petrified Luna as they did so.

Luna could but now brace herself, and as the first of the evil dead bore down on her, the hollow orbits of their eyes seething with hatred and vengeance, she plaintively cried out to the G, "Creator of the universe, if I have offended you, then take me! But leave my sister and all our system in peace! Aaaarghhh!"

At that precise moment, from the right side of the blackened, oozing mass that had been her sister, a stunning and intense light suddenly appeared and grew; a sharp, piercing blue light, whose rays sliced through the writhing army of the dead, cleaving and scattering and withering them as it cleared the ring of fire that still encompassed Gaia.

The skull too started to writhe as if in agony, as the light arced towards them, bleaching the vile shroud from Gaia's surface as it went. The darkness then rallied and tried to fight the blue light, as the scattered legions of the dead sought to regroup and envelop Luna once more.

Luna repeated her prayer as the light suddenly diminished again as it moved behind Gaia, from whom the blackness had been removed at one side, and Luna could once again see some of the blue and the white of her sister.

And, as if in answer to her second prayer, another light miraculously appeared from almost the same place as the first. This light was, however, much less intense, and glowed a deep red. But, despite its diminished brilliance, it had the same effect, and caused the darkness to recoil and disperse even more violently. Luna watched in astonished relief as more of Gaia's glorious beauty was returned to her, as the darkness was driven back and the ghosts of the dead dissolved before her. And before she knew it, the brilliant blue sapphire reappeared on the other side of Gaia, and both the lights acted together to cleanse and restore her beloved sister.

And there, suddenly, was Gaia, just as she had almost always been. Once more she was resplendent in her blues and whites, and greens and browns; those wonderful living colours which again reached into Luna with the all compassionate grace and warmth that they had always carried with them. Luna still felt as if she was shaking uncontrollably, but was further relieved to see that all the stars were once again all present and glistening in their multitudes, just as they had always done. In the distance, to one side of Gaia, she could see Mars and his boys; and to the other, and now receding from them, the vibrant blue sparkle that was Venus.

"Is Luna all right now?" Mars enquired from afar.

"Er? Well? I think so?" Gaia replied. "Hold on a moment."

"Luna, my dear," Gaia gently asked. "How are you? Have you come back to us? Please say that you have."

What a strange question, Luna thought, before she replied, "Yes sister, I am fine, I think. I do feel a bit sick and wobbly, mind. I think I had a bit of a bad dream? And I feel so tired, and have no idea why? But, yes, as far as I can tell I am fine. Back to you? What do you mean, back to you?"

"You do not remember?"

"Remember what? I remember that a lot your forests were burning. I hope that has all stopped now. And we were about to sort through all our recent work with Mars and his boys and Eureka and her clan. We should get back to that, as I want to know how you are, and what we might now know about what is going to happen to you if those apes keep behaving the way they have been?"

"Yes, Mars, I think she is OK," Gaia answered to their red friend, "I cannot thank you and Venus enough. We are forever in your debt," she continued.

"Oh, I am so glad," Mars replied "You gave us such a terrible fright, Luna. Even the gassers were worried about you. We are so happy that you are with us once again. I am thinking a period of convalescence is very much in order, mind, for all of us. I am shattered, as is Venus. She had to draw on all her powers to get you out of that funk you were in. I helped out as best I could, but it is really her you owe a debt of gratitude to."

"What? Venus? Powers? What are you all talking about?" Luna asked. "And why can't I hear anything from the apes, why is everything so suddenly quiet? I can hear the deep space rhythms all right, but nothing from the hominids. Has something happened to them?" She paused for a moment, seemingly puzzled, before she continued, "Hang on! The stars are not where they should be? I mean I can see they are all there, but… Oh!"

And once more Gaia tenderly shifted her clouds before saying,

"Ah! I see you understand. Yes! She's back, my sharp little sister!" she then joyfully announced to Mars.

Luna said nothing for a little while as she studied the cosmos, and thought for a moment, before enquiring, "If I am not mistaken, I seem to have lost the best part of one of our cycles round the Sun somehow? What happened?"

"Yes. About eight and a bit of your orbits round me, give or take. But let's not worry about that just now. And let's not worry about all that damned data, and emissions, or any analysis for the moment. You need to rest and recuperate for a bit. We all do, as Mars says. As to the apes, they are still there making all their noise and mess, though they too have had a bit of an interesting time of late. We can but hope that they might actually learn some lessons this time. The reason that you cannot hear them is down to Venus. She has, and I do not yet understand quite how, put in some sort of filters for you to keep them out, at least until you have recovered your strength a bit and might have rebuilt your own defences against them. Next time she comes by she is going to have a look, and we are all going to have a little chat. If she thinks you have recovered sufficiently, she will start removing these blocks and give us both some training so we can moderate our exposure to all the hominid cacophony as we see fit. She really is quite something, as it turns out, and we have much to learn from her."

Luna was utterly dazed, and as tired as she could ever remember being. It was strange to think that, for the first time ever, she had contrived to lose the best part of a whole solar cycle. What could have caused that? And what had she been doing for about eight of her cycles around her sister? And Venus? What on Gaia was that about?

The sudden quiet in the hominid part of the spectrum, was both decidedly strange, but oddly comforting, as were the deep space melodies, which she had not listened to for some good time. She had almost forgotten what such quiet tranquillity was like. To suddenly have it back, after over a hundred Gaian cycles of the bedlam of the hominid broadcasting, was odd, but she understood that she really did need a bit of peace and quiet and rest for a bit.

More than that, she was a sensible enough little moon, if a mysteriously shaken and confused one, to recognise that, whatever had happened in the last few of her cycles, she did not need to know right now. She should heed Gaia and Mars, and trust that she would find everything out eventually. All she wanted right now was to enjoy this calm, for as long as it might last, and to be with her sister.

Luna spent the next few of her orbits enjoying the quiet, chatting with Gaia, and regaining her strength. Gaia, being all too conscious of what had transpired, insisted that they take things slowly, as the whole affair had taken a considerable toll on her as well, not to mention the rest of the system. During this time, and with all the inherent compassion and dexterity of her sister in play, Luna came to understand what, from the perspective of everyone else, had happened; and compassion was the right word, as Gaia had very much suffered alongside Luna during those unheard of, and frankly terrifying, few months. Luna could still not remember a thing, but from the slow but steady drip-feeding of information that came her way, she came to understand what had transpired during her 'absence'.

Gaia's precious forests, she was disheartened to hear, were still being set ablaze and destroyed all over her sister just as they had been a few of her cycles previously; and, as ever, all as a result, directly or indirectly, of the sapiens' stupidity and their greedy, myopic, ways. However, the most significant event that had come to pass during her absence was that Life itself seemed to have tried again — and this, to Luna, seemed to be its fourth or fifth attempt in the last few decades — to send the hominids a clear warning, in regards to how they were behaving, in the only way it knew how.

From the land of that great wall, at least according to what the available evidence had suggested up to now, Life had manifested a new virus. A new virus that had made very rapid and efficient use of the globalised trade and transport networks of which the apes were so proud, to inveigle and then disseminate itself throughout the hominid world, causing chaos as it went. Not that it was the most deadly, or even the most infectious disease that Life had ever manifested. It had, however, enough of both of these qualities to clearly expose all of the fragilities, inequities, and wrong-headedness of those economic and political systems that the apes had contrived to blindly bind themselves to in the name of profit and growth and money, as they had gone about their business of greedily despoiling Gaia.

And when Luna had recovered enough strength, she cast her analytical eye over the numbers, saw the patterns, and understood the implications of what was, for the apes, still very much an ongoing situation, as they continued to battle one of the simplest, yet one of the most slippery and agile, emanations of Life.

Impressed and depressed in equal measure, she could but raise a sigh and hope that, for once, the lessons that Life was trying to teach its most intelligent, yet equally stupid, progeny, might this time be learned, before she returned to trying to understand what had happened to her, and why.

She discovered that she had experienced, to use a hominid term, a 'burn-out', the causes of which were manifold, but all of which had their foundations in the aberrant, and sometimes frankly awful, behaviour of the apes.

She did not care much for the term 'burn-out' though. For starters, it reminded her of the asteroids, the meteorites and, most of all, of those lonely, fatalistic wanderers, the comets. Then, there seemed to be the suggestion, which to her was implicit in this term, that it was she who had 'burned out' and, therefore, the responsibility for this lay with her alone. For sure, she had to shoulder some of the burden for the way everything had gone lately — and some of the details that Gaia relayed to her were truly shocking — but was this really the case?

In her opinion, her responsibility lay only in caring for her sister, and all of the beautiful Life she hosted, even the humans. She was, after all, partly responsible for the rise of Life itself; and though Life had arisen from a decidedly unusual, not to say unlikely, amalgamation of things, of which she was but one, she loved it as she loved Gaia. True, Life had been a bit of a bastard insofar as how it had been conceived, and they still did not understand all of the details in that respect, and the pinnacle of that Life had latterly shown itself to be a rather stupid, selfish, and greedy bastard, in a number of different ways. But, as with her responsibility, this was not the whole story.

Unlike the roving vagabonds of the cosmos, she felt that she did have, and had made, a choice. She could have chosen not to care at all, and to look away when things had started to go bad. She could have simply turned her back, let things play out, and perhaps come back when the offending infestation had contrived to remove itself from existence through its own stupidity, as seemed increasingly likely;

had been obliterated by external cosmic intervention; or, driven to extinction, albeit accidently, by Gaia and her still unpredictable innards. To have turned her back on Life, and the apes, would have been, in many ways, far easier on her and everyone else.

But how could she have done such a feckless and cowardly thing? To do that, she reasoned, would be to deny all the love and hopeful compassion with which the G had blessed her. In short, it would have been to deny her very essence; something that seemed as impossible as it was absurd. Finally, she realised that the choice she considered she had, though a choice it remained, was only of that sort that had been famously offered by a certain Mr Hobson, long-time deceased native of the funny little island. How could she have done otherwise?

As such, might it not be fairer to say that, far from suffering a 'burn-out', she had in fact been 'burnt out' by everything that had come to pass recently? Was not the true source of her distress, not to say that of everyone else, the increasingly awful and selfish behaviour of the sapiens? Behaviour that at first, she had only heard about, but that latterly she had been forced to witness, amidst the noise and babble that for a hundred cycles the apes had bestowed upon the locality.

That she could do nothing but watch what the apes continued to do to each other, the rest of Life, and Gaia, had been a torture in itself. Had not the utter helplessness that she had had to endure, simply as she would not turn her back on Life, or her sister, not been the fundamental reason that she had had her 'breakdown'? Or, had it been her reaction to that sense of impotence, allied to the growing horror and stupidity that she had been obliged to contemplate, which had been the real cause of what had recently happened?

"Paragon of animals, indeed!" she thought to herself, wondering how many of the apes knew that famous line. Quite a few, she imagined, as the author of the line, and the brilliance of his writing, was one of those very rare things that the apes actually seemed to be able to agree upon, even if they could not agree as to whether the ape in question had indeed written all the works that bore his name. But, she pondered further, how many of the hominids knew the line that followed? What was it now? She rifled through the gargantuan encyclopedia that she had become in respect of all things Gaian, and true to form, she wrestled it from within.

"And yet to me, what is this quintessence of dust? Man delights not me; no, nor woman neither."

Yes, she thought to herself, that about sums it up, thinking further that it was also very true to say that lately she had very much 'lost her mirth'.

How lucky was she, though, to have Gaia, Mars and his strange little band, and even Venus, it seemed, as friends? Friends who really cared about her and who had, according to her sister, in the case of Mars and Venus, placed themselves in considerable danger to drag her from whatever abyss she had fallen into.

Venus? Now that was a real mystery; and one that she now really wanted to understand, even though she could not but help feel rather apprehensive about the imminent return of her saviour. What was she going to say to her to explain herself and her behaviour? She was still racked with guilt concerning that moment all those decades ago, when she had joined in with Gaia in abusing her to such a degree that no one had heard a peep out of Venus since that time. Until now that was.

Had that act been the first sign, she wondered, that she had already started her slide into some dark void of madness? A madness that was the result of all the worry for her sister, all the noise and images that constantly battered her senses, and all the obsessive information gathering and analysis that she had, in desperation, submitted herself and the others to?

Was that it? Was that her sin? To have been driven to the point of obsession regarding what these creatures were doing?

Lost in her thoughts, she rounded Gaia as she had always done, to be startled by a voice; a voice that she was not familiar with, but which resonated in a rather odd way within her; a voice that was beautiful, tender, and compassionate.

"Hello Luna. How are you doing, my dear?" it said.

Summoning up her courage, as she came out from behind her sister, she then gazed toward the Sun to find that Venus, resplendent in her sapphire shimmer — a shimmer that now touched her in some strange but gentle way — had appeared, and was heading toward them.

"Don't worry," the voice continued. "We have much to discuss, you and I. But all is well, and all will be well. I promise you."

The little moon found she could not utter a word, so taken aback that this was Venus? Could it really be the same Venus who for eons had been that vicious and terrible harridan that everyone had had to put up with?

And then, as if reading her thoughts, the voice said, "Yes. It is. At least in form, if not substance; and I am delighted to meet you after such a long, long time."

Perplexed, Luna looked down to Gaia, but she seemed preoccupied with something and had not noticed that Venus had appeared from behind the Sun. Then she realized that the voice, if one could describe it as such, appeared to be inside of her, and that Venus had not actually said a word as she continued her serene passage towards them?

"Don't say anything," Venus continued, "You do not have to. Just feel. You are very special moon, my dear. Not every celestial body is capable of what we are doing now. Indeed, until recently, my own madness had made me forget that I could; and then there is Mars, who for reasons

I shall not go into now, had chosen to forget for a very, very, long time. That is until he had to remember in order to come to your aid."

Ordinarily, the little moon would have been profoundly disturbed by what was now happening. She sensed deep within, however, that there was nothing to worry about, and the mention of Mars conjured up in her a sort of vague memory, one of a distant glowing red light that somehow seemed to be a partner to the brilliant blue of Venus.

"So what is going on? What is it that we are now doing? Is this what the apes call telepathy?" Luna then tried to feel, rather than state, in compliance with what Venus had just relayed to her.

"No," the voice replied ever so gently, "not telepathy as they conceive of it. We are empaths, and you are a very powerful one, not that anyone, not even you, had ever realized, it seems. It is a great gift, perhaps the greatest that the G has bestowed upon any of us; that ability to understand and communicate entirely through feeling alone. But, as with all great talents, it can be double-sided, and that flipside is what you have recently experienced. Your innate ability to feel and understand, especially in respect of your sister, is so strong, that in the face of the unrelentingly crass behaviour of those apes, you turned it upon yourself. Subconsciously, you tried to absolve your sister of all their sins, so that she could be free of them. Such nobility, such willingness to self-sacrifice, this system has never seen, and you almost paid a terrible price for it. Indeed, so strong an empath are you that it took the combined efforts of myself and Mars to bring you back."

Even if Luna had wanted to say anything she could not. Instead, she reflected profoundly on what Venus was communicating to her, and deep within her she found that there was truth in what Venus was saying.

Then she felt, "But what am I to do? Something has to be done about the apes. Someone needs to make them see the error of their ways before they destroy everything, including themselves."

"Yes, my dear Luna. But we have no agency in these matters, and the first thing you need to do if you really want to help your sister is to learn how to protect yourself, and I am bound by my own nature and experience to ensure that you do. These are unseemly times, and I fear that things may well get worse before they get better. And, if nothing else, I owe you a great debt."

"A great debt?" Luna thought. "What debt?"

"Well, Luna," Venus replied, "were it not for you, I should still be stuck within that terrible anguished cage that the G saw fit to imprison me within for so long."

Now Luna was thoroughly befuddled, and sensing this Venus continued.

"That event of decades ago, the one you feel so guilty about. There one wherein you directed all your inner anger and resentment at what was happening to your sister, at me?"

"Oh!" Luna, thought, or was it felt, back, "Yes, I am so, so sorry for that. I do not know what came over me, or Gaia."

"No Luna. Do not apologise. It seems that the universe sometimes does move in extremely mysterious ways. Somehow, so great was your rage, and so great was the passion and love for your sister that lay behind it, that it scythed through my own madness and broke the spell that had immured me for so long. I was free at last, thanks to you. But, after such a long time, I was so weak and ashamed that I could but spend the intervening years in contemplation of what I had become and why. That was until Mars — at your request so I understand — plucked up the courage to approach me and ask about what had happened to my atmosphere all those eons ago. You have no idea just how hard that was for him, but being the honourable and caring wanderer he has always been, he did so nonetheless. Since then, and as and when our respective orbits permitted us to meet behind the Sun, he has been helping me recover, counselling me if you will. And now it is my turn to help you as much as I am able.

"But what about Gaia? She needs help too, and I am not sure I am comfortable speaking, or is it thinking? Or feeling? Without her knowing. That's not right. I cannot go behind her back."

"Oh! What a truly beautiful moon you are, Luna, your first thoughts are always for someone else. Do not worry so.

Empathy exists in all us sentient astral bodies to a greater or lesser degree, and Gaia too is capable of joining us if she wants to. But right now, if you take a second to feel, you will understand that she wants us to have a moment together before we resume with that more usual form of communication."

Luna did as Venus had suggested, and from below she suddenly felt a loving complicity welling up from beneath her. She understood immediately, and felt happy.

"You see," Venus continued. "We all have our language, even the apes have gotten that far. However, language, however advanced it may be, is really only ever an approximation to meaning. Once one recognises this, one is forced to ask as to if and where absolute meaning might reside? Some seek it in the precision of logic, and mathematics, and analysis, and it is true to say that there is much to be recommended therein. Of themselves, however, these are but tools that cannot explain many things, such as what we are doing now. Therefore, one must go beyond those things as well, and to feel; that most profound, mysterious, and dangerous, of all the gifts of the G, to those who are sentient enough to realise it. Your sister knows, even if she is nowhere near as gifted in this respect as you are, and even if she may not have understood it in such an explicit manner until now. But then again, she has been blessed with another, most remarkable — not to say unique, as far as we are aware — gift; that of the Life she hosts.

"Mars understands these things as well, as do even some of the apes. Not enough perhaps but, as we both know, these are hard roads to follow.

"As to the apes, they will either find their way, or they will not. But, irrespective of what they decide to do, and how they might end up, that is a choice that they have the power to make, even now.

"None of us may have what the hominids, in their rather absolutist formulation, describe as 'free will'. We cannot change, by our own volition, the paths that the G has decreed we must follow. This much the creator proscribes to us. But this does not mean that we have no choice as to how we conduct ourselves. And in this respect, I have been given a second chance, thanks to you and your sister.

"What is it they say down there?" she continued. "To err is human, but to forgive is divine. Very typical of them to claim a universal truth as their own, but there is wisdom to be found in those sentiments. Perhaps more important, however, is to learn from our mistakes, lest they be repeated and compounded.

"As such, Luna, do not worry about your sister so, irrespective of what the apes decide to do. Perhaps they will make it to the next level of consciousness, and from that illumination, will be able to correct their aberrant ways before it is too late. And perhaps they will not, and they will cease to be. That must be their choice, and must be to them alone. Whatever they do, however, Gaia, and you, and I, and Mars and all the others will go on.

"We still have our work cut out with Mercury, mind. By times, and since you freed me, I have touched him too, and understood what an anguished and tortured soul he is. That, however, is a story for another time, save to say that I have also realized that it is beyond my power alone to help him. Equally, I also believe that, in time, the four of us together can still reach him and bring him back; and it would be utterly wrong of us to forget about him, would it not?

"As to your sister and her Life. Life on Gaia will continue no matter what the apes contrive to do next, of that I am convinced. Yours is a very different, more temperate orbit, compared to mine. What's more, in the plants, and the trees, and the seas, you have many powerful allies amidst the cornucopia of Life that your sister hosts, great legions who could correct whatever the apes do if they were but left in peace to get on with their work. As you know well, Life has more than shown itself to be tough, resourceful, and extremely tenacious; and who knows, given another few million cycles, what new heights it may reach, with or without the hominids?"

With that, Venus stopped, and suggested that they should now go and have a chat with Gaia, give her a look over, and see how she was doing. And as they did so, she started to explain to them both how she had done what she had done to Luna, and how it could, as and when Luna was ready, be undone. She also explained that it would be necessary for Luna to confront those images and memories, such that she might free herself from any possibility of a relapse. To willingly forget what had happened was equivalent to denial; and a denial of the facts, however difficult they might be, was to deny the possibility of any evolution toward a better future.

She also told them that Mars had been dispatched to teach the others the techniques that they had been quietly developing behind the Sun over these last decades. With Panic and Fear, they had come up with what appeared to be a curious mix of mathematics and meditation to filter out whatever the apes were chucking at them through the void of space. Through these means, she hoped that whoever wished to return to the tranquility of the cosmos could do so as and when they pleased. That was to be her gift to their system; one that she hoped would, in some way, make up for those eons of her own awful behaviour.

Enraptured by the revelation that was the inner beauty of Venus, Luna, and Gaia could but listen, and then also feel that, irrespective of what the apes might contrive to do in the future, they would indeed go on together. That they would all go on as part of a complete and balanced system wherein they would all feel for, and look after, one another.

A little while later, and just before Venus would be compelled by the G to take her leave of them for a little while before returning for their next session, Venus asked Luna a question.

"Now that we have established the whys and wherefores of what recently happened to you. And now that we understand that what came to pass can only be seen as a positive reflection upon your compassionate and empathetic nature, to which no guilt should be ascribed, I might ask you, Luna: if you could speak directly to the apes right now, what might you say to them?"

To this, Luna thought for a while before replying, "Well, I cannot tell you all the things that I have wanted to express in respect of, and indeed to, the hominids. Over the cycles they have been so damned exasperating, and many of their actions, even today, so demented, stupid, and just plain wrong."

"By times, I shall admit that I have just wanted to scream at them precisely what selfish, greedy fuckwits they have become. You have no idea what enraged soliloquys they have brought to my mind. But, all told, what good would that do, even if such a direct exhortation were even possible? For all their stupidity, they are a nuanced, if prideful, species, and the use of such blunt force would only be counter-productive, I think."

"Instead, I now find myself reminded of when they first came to visit me, but a moment ago. Not the instant they did, you understand, as by then I could not enjoy that experience, even though I had longed for it ever since Life appeared upon my sister. No, what comes to mind is something one of their leaders had proclaimed almost seven solar cycles before they came, not long before he was murdered. What he said was this: "'We choose to go to the Moon. We choose to go to the Moon. We choose to go to the Moon in this decade and do the other things, not because they are easy, but because they are hard; because that goal will serve to organize and measure the best of our energies and skills, because that challenge is one that we are willing to accept, one we are unwilling to postpone, and one we intend to win, and the others, too.'

"With that in mind, I would simply ask hominids the following: If that was the case then, and you did pay me a visit less than seven years after that proclamation, then why can you not resolve to apply that same inspirational, can-do, will-do philosophy to the preservation of your own environment, which is to say, my sister, and indeed yourselves?

"For sure, you have already stored up a whole heap of trouble for yourselves. Gaia's atmosphere and oceans can take a lot, and are so massive that they are intrinsically slow to react. But do not mistake that inertia for indifference. Once they do start to move, and I sense that this may have already begun, you will understand their power; power enough to humble you and, if necessary, smite you down.

"Is it not utterly ludicrous that you achieved what you achieved back then as a result of simple, but focused, national pride? Yet you cannot contrive to have the common sense or the humility to realise that what faces you now is an imminent and global problem of your own making? A problem, moreover, that can still be solved, if you were to have the courage and the intelligence to come together and act now?

"If you cannot do that for yourselves, can you not contrive to do so for the sake of your children, and your children's children? The future of your whole species is at risk when it need not be so, had you but the sense, strength, and humility to act as one, in all our best interests. Perhaps, if you could manage that, even if just for your own sake, then I might consider your appropriation of the epithet 'sapiens' as in some way valid.

"Yes, these things will be hard… but was anything ever worth doing that was not? So like the man said, go organise and measure the best of your energies and skills, and accept the challenge to rectify that for which you are responsible. But, whatever you do, do not keep prevaricating. Be courageous enough to be unwilling to postpone what needs to be done; as to postpone those changes, which are within your capacity to achieve, will be the end of you.

"All said and done, and in spite of everything, I should rather not have to mourn you as just one more of Life's failed experiments. You are, I believe, and in spite of everything, rather more than that.

"That, I think," concluded Luna, "is what I should like to say to them if I could."

"Ah Luna, would that they had but a fraction of your sagacity, compassion, and love! That they might indeed take heed of the view of their moon," Venus felt to them both, seeming to shimmer even more brilliantly than usual as she did so.

"I will be back in a bit," she added, "but in between times, have a feel of this, I think it might clarify a few things," as under the benevolent but implacable impulse of the G, she once more took her leave of them.

Luna did not have time to reply, as she gazed upon the gently receding Venus, before she felt something stir deep inside of her. Happily, this was not the infernal trembling she had recently experienced, and which she had no desire to experience again. No, this felt gentle and warm, yet imbued with great power; and, as it rose up within her, it resolved itself into something she recognised and loved! That most wondrous and beautiful of all of humanity's creations, music! Symphonic music!

More than that, she immediately knew the piece! A work that had been created almost two hundred Gaian solar cycles ago, but which she had only been able to experience sometime later, when the humans had started to broadcast into space. From her vast repository of knowledge, she permitted what she knew of this monumental work, along with the images of the author, to appear as the first movement began with its curiously tentative opening phrases; phrases that, to the little moon, had always suggested the act of contemplation that preceded the genesis of a great idea.

Such a stern, angry looking, ape? His countenance, and apparent demeanour, so completely at odds with the beauty that he had created during his brief existence, she felt, as she mused upon the images she had of this sapiens, and the music took on a definitive form which began to envelope her in a rapturous delight. This revolutionary ape, who by the time he had created it had entirely lost his ability to hear, seemed now to be trying to speak to her through his music; music that had to have been created through the purity of his feeling alone. "Was this Venus's reason for giving this particular gift?" she wondered momentarily.

Luna allowed herself to submit to the wonderful and compassionate force of the evolving architectures of form which washed over, and then permeated into her, as the great ape conducted her through his imagined Universe. A Universe that — bang! — did suddenly burst into existence, just as they had always thought, and the sapiens had seemed to have confirmed through their acquired understanding of physics and astronomy.

And from that sudden beginning it rapidly careered hither and thither before, in the middle of the movement, it changed. The music, or so Luna thought, then started to speak of the meticulous dexterity and precision of the G, as the work of shaping and ordering the universe was attended to. The logic of creation demands harmony, just as the logic of music demands harmony, the ape seemed to be saying to her.

"Yes! Of Course!" she thought, now almost delirious and feeling herself seeming to ascend somewhere, as the second movement began with what seemed like an abrupt cosmic intervention, but which rapidly thereafter started to run in a free-flowing manner.

"Molto vivace!" Luna found herself exclaiming, before rendering this musical instruction, without, she thought, too much linguistic chicanery, into 'full of Life!' OMG! The deaf, dead ape was now speaking to her of Gaia and the Life that she had had a role in creating and directing along its way: how it had appeared, reached out, and then bloomed and diversified; how it was periodically interrupted and had to start again; and how it had radically altered their lives with its stunning pace of change.

The beginning of the third movement then magically conjured up the brilliance of the light of the Sun as it emerged from behind her sister. The music now spoke of the glorious dawn that was the Life as it organised itself, and indeed her sister, into a unique, beautiful, balanced, and self-sustaining, architecture of such majestic form. It also spoke to her, with its more relaxed tempo, of the love they had for this Life and how she and her sister had gradually accommodated to the increased rates of change that had, by this point, come to dominate their existence.

Those ideas again: architecture and form? Yes, the logic of Life demanded harmony as well. Was this what the ape was revealing to her? That everything was intimately connected and driven by this implacable reasoning? As did not form presuppose logic, and therefore, reason and meaning? If so, was this the true purpose of the universe? To create the harmony of form from which meaning and truth may subsequently be derived?

Luna let these thoughts dissolve into her as she gazed down in awe and love at her sister. She then looked to Venus, and gave her thanks for this delightful present, and then to distant Mars and his boys, who were such steadfast and wonderful friends. Lastly, she gazed beyond the Sun to the vast, endless expanse of the cosmos. The grace and serenity of this third movement was so beautiful she briefly found herself wishing that she could stay in this wondrous form-space forever, as the gentle waves of ape strings and ape horns carried her blissfully along.

But, as she knew well, she could not. The great ape, had not been content even with this level of harmonised complexity and, just as the G had done eons beforehand, he had demanded more. As night followed day for the sapiens, the ethereal delights of the third movement eventually had to give way to the fourth, in a staccato burst that prefigured the rise of something new. A new form, within which there appeared to be expressions of both light and dark as elements of the orchestra seemed to challenge and compete with one another before they came together into a simple, yet forceful, and irrepressibly striving, theme. Luna then understood what was now being presented to her. It was the rise of self-awareness, in the form of the sapiens and their unique voice. And with their rise came two further new concepts. The first was freedom; the freedom to choose. The second was responsibility; responsibility for the choices made, and the consequences that might follow from them.

Yes, Luna could see that there was great joy to be had in this radical new departure, and could not but help herself singing out loud.

"O! Fruende, nicht diese Töne!
Sondern laßt uns angenehmere anstimmen,
und freudenvollere.
Freude!
Freude!"

And as she sang, it then dawned upon her that the dead, deaf, stern-of-countenance composer, was a sapiens in the truest sense of the word, and that he had rather more fully understood the ramifications of this new enlightenment than the rest of his species appeared to have done even now.

"My G!" she thought. What a revelation! How had she not understood this before? The first words that a human voice had ever been permitted to utter within a symphonic creation constituted a plea on the behalf of the composer! One that was both recognition of the possibility of freedom and choice, and a warning to use these gifts wisely and to choose better ways to be!

More than that, Luna sensed something else amidst the staggering beauty of these human voices and the instrumental forms that whirled around her. Something more recent, that she felt was profoundly related, but the precise source of which eluded her. As they sang of Elysium, Luna found herself once more staring down at her sister; and she did see seas of green; and she did see skies of blue and clouds of white; and she could see the blessed day, and the dark sacred night; and she had a further epiphany.

Gaia was not just a wonderful sister. She was the Elysium, not to mention all those other mythical paradises that the upright apes like to convince themselves had either been lost or were the sole preserve of the dead, they were singing about! She then immediately comprehended that the little system bequeathed to them by the G was not just some inconsequential and non-descript backwater to the universe. No! It was a unique and very, very, special place! And with this unexpected enlightenment, a further great wave of joy spread through the little moon such that she thought she was beaming as bright as the Sun, as the human voices, and their harmony with the rest of the orchestra, grew, both in volume and complexity, to carry her with them!

How had she contrived not to understand this until now, she wondered? And why on Gaia could the sapiens not see this, nor understand the great gift of the ability to choose that had been bequeathed to them?

In the case of the sapiens, all the work she had been engaged in over the last decades with Gaia, and Mars and his curious collective, informed her that a monumental choice was soon going to be forced upon them. A potentially terrible reckoning was due, irrespective, or perhaps as a result of, their inability to accept the terms of the bargain the universe had implicitly struck with them: that they should act in harmony with everything else, and that they would be held responsible for their choices.

For, if the logic of Life and the universe demanded harmony, then Life and the Universe at large would act to promote such harmony, and to remove those elements which could not, or would not, be harmonized, would it not?

For every action, there was an equal and opposite re-action. This was a fundamental law of the universe, one which the apes had, through reason, come to understand. Yet somehow they seemed to be intent upon ignoring this axiom, or restricting it only to the realms of physics and physical motion. But were not existence, the universe, and Life itself, forms of motion, and therefore subject to this most profound of truths? The apes had reason, and from that, they possessed the freedom to choose; and that choice, and the responsibility that accompanied it, was to them alone.

With that thought, and as the final movement of the gift that Venus had bestowed upon her came to its climatic end, Luna felt the last residues of guilt regarding the apes and what they had been doing to her sister melt away into the vacuum of space; and, for the first time in what seemed to her a very long time, she felt at peace.

She very much hoped the apes would, even at this late stage, see sense, and correct their ways. They had the science and the technology, of that Luna was in no doubt, but did they have the comprehension and wherewithal to come together and enter into that higher collective consciousness from which the harmony demanded of all things by the universe might be attained?

"Oh!" she felt to herself, "that they all might go forward together into that most joyous and greatest of all adventures."

But, if they did not, and they chose to remove themselves from existence, she had now finally understood something. She understood that she, Gaia, and the Life that they loved and cared for so much, would find a way to carry on irrespective, just as they always had since Life had blessed them with its presence in this most special of all the places in the cosmos.

Acknowledgements

I am extremely grateful of those friends of mine who have taken the time to read through, and critically comment upon, versions of this story: Elizabeth Stone-Matho, Adelaide Calbry-Muzyka, Petr Šot, Aleta Thomas, Hilary Newton, Gerald Bauer, Lucie Batchelor, Tamara Vugrin, Werner Marti, Arik Beck, Cynthia Ashperger, Hannes Frey, and Andrea Blankenship (who also came up with the concept for the cover design). I cannot thank you adequately enough.

I might also like to thank those who have put up with me talking about this story whenever the opportunity presented itself; and no doubt, irrespective of whether anyone wanted me too. Specifically: Amy Knorpp, Laure Caillat, Marco Di Michiel, Amrita Singh-Morgan, and Seb Wendt, along with anyone else that I have bothered regarding it.

Then, there are the places where I have found that I can write. It may seem a bit odd to acknowledge places, but a suitable environment appears just as important as anything else. As such, I cite: Azzuro (http://azzurro.ch/wp/home/) Moby Hicks pop up beer shop (https://mobyhicks.ch/), along with Diego, Cyrille, and all those who I have met there, and who have made me so welcome upon their terrace. To them I would add my mother's kitchen, and the Schweizerische Bundesbahnen (https://www.sbb.ch/), whose restaurant cars I have found to be rather amenable to writing stuff.

I should also cite that most noble of emanations of the interweb, Wikipedia (https://www.wikipedia.org/), as an excellent first point of inquiry regarding many things. I might also cite the no doubt less noble, but equally useful, resource that is Youtube (https://www.youtube.com/). I am also indebted to the work of those behind more specialist websites, most specifically, https://earthsky.org/

Lastly, I should very much like to thank David Haviland who, rather by chance, I met via Reedsy (https://reedsy.com). David has proved himself an excellent editor and I am extremely indebted to him for his guidance and instruction in realising this little work.

Printed in Great Britain
by Amazon

13696591R00093